A Paris (

BY

AXEL FORRESTER

**FLYING
START**

PRESS

A Cataloguing in Publication record for this book is available from the British Library
Cover design by Axel Forrester

ISBN: 9781739653996

Chapter One

When I stepped off the train at Gare du Nord, I reached for my wallet, only to discover it was gone. Checking the pocket of my backpack I found that the keys to my flat were also missing. Next, I fumbled inside my coat pocket. No passport. So expertly had I been pick-pocketed that I had finally arrived in Paris with no identification, no money, no credit cards, and no keys to my friend's flat. As the shock of this spread across my body, despair set in, and I lowered myself right there on the platform to a crouching position with my arms around my suitcase and backpack.

'Welcome to Paris!' said an evil, scratchy voice inside my head, like the one you'd imagine a gargoyle to have.

OK then, I told myself, as I brought my luggage closer to my chest. *The rules here are different.* I'd thought that growing up in Los Angeles, I'd be somewhat prepared for a big place like Paris, but I was wrong.

Of course, I hadn't been on trains much in LA. I had a car like millions of other people in California. You're safe in a car, with the doors locked.

Katie did warn me about pickpockets, which is why I had put important stuff in different places, but that didn't matter. Somehow it was all gone! Keys! Wallet! Passport! I was trembling now, hugging my backpack tightly.

'*Snap out of it!*' yelled my inner travel warrior, jerking me to attention. *You've been to CHINA and back again. You can handle PARIS. Pull yourself together, man!* Like any hero in a tight spot, I knew there'd been a big loss, but now it was time to take inventory of what I *did* have, of what was left. To my great relief my two cameras, one analog, one digital, were still around my neck, which was probably why they hadn't been stolen. The other thing of value I had left was my cell phone in my back pocket. Was it time to call Katie? She'd get this fixed in no time. But it seemed awfully soon to call for help. Some part of my manly pride said, *NO, Grant Decker. You can figure this out on your own. At least your phone works here. You have options.*

One thing I had remembered to do was write down the emergency numbers from my credit cards and store them in another place. I reached into my shirt pocket. Yes. It was still there, the little piece of paper with the lost or stolen numbers. *Smart man!* All I had to do now was get out of the station, get a signal, and make the call.

I looked all around me, as I stood up on shaky legs. Now, where was the sign showing the way out to the street? *Exit* in America. *Way Out* in Britain. What was it in French? There were so many tunnels and signs. I didn't understand a word on any of them. Katie had tried to get me to practice a few French phrases, but I'd paid no attention. I was only going to be here four weeks. My pronunciation of French was awful. Might as well not embarrass myself.

All the signs seemed to lead to some place called SORTIE. Sortie here. Sortie there. Oh, come on! They couldn't *all* be going to this SORTIE place unless ... maybe it was a vast circular road around this insanely large train station.

The crowds from the train were long gone. More trains pulled up, more people got out, repeatedly. In waves. I watched them. All these faces. Preoccupied. Tired. Worried.

3

But none of them lost. Leaves letting go of branches and hurrying on the wind. They all knew exactly where they were going. I should follow someone. But who?

In one of the quiet lulls, I noticed the only people hanging about here. They were not waiting. Purposeful, yet relaxed. Unhurried. These were old men. Wearing ragged suits, they needed a shave, lounging on benches reading newspapers or moving very slowly down the platform, clutching a tall dark bottle by the neck. One man was fast asleep on the tiled floor, snoring, his hair straining in all directions, as if trying to escape his head. Two other men were facing each other on a bench, deep in conversation.

Moving toward them, I noticed they had stopped talking when they saw me and now frowned. They appeared to be offended by *my* appearance. When I opened my mouth to speak, I had to stop. What was the French word for hello? There was only my stunned silence. What I did was wave. They turned back to their discussion. To my American ear, their French sounded refined, civilized, and intimidating.

There was the swoosh and flutter of pigeon wings, darting above my head, a sound I knew and should have taken comfort in, but instead I held fast to my cameras and the fear of all I didn't know. As I watched, they flew up into a shaft of light, coming from a high window. And there it was, my impulse to take a photo, only I'd missed my chance, standing there without a tongue.

There was an odor. Sweat. Old socks. Beer. My shoulder was tapped, and I jumped, gripping my two cameras to my chest. No one was going to take these off me. If it came to blows, then so be it! As I turned, one of these men who hung around stood there staring at me with rheumy eyes and a down turned mouth, a sad clown from a distant time. He spoke softly to me, trying not to scare me, but I understood nothing. I waited for him to put his hand out for money, but he didn't. It took me a moment to realize that he felt sorry for me and was trying to help me somehow. He spoke again, slowly, kindly, as if to a child, or a small animal. Again, I it meant nothing to me. I tried out my voice. Squeaky and apologizing.

'I'm sorry, I don't speak French. I'm very sorry.' None of the French phrases Katie had so thoughtfully made me write down came to mind.

'Lost?' he said, in English. There was a sparkle in his eye.

And now, at the sound of my own language, my heart swelled up like a balloon in simple, fragile hope.

'You speak English?' I almost grabbed his hand, but sensibly pulled it back and bowed instead. 'Thank you!

Could you please show me the way out of this place? Way out? Exit?'

'Sortie?'

I blushed.

'Sortie means exit?'

'Oui.' *And that means, yes.* I was remembering now.

Some part of my brain finally lit up. Flashbacks came to me, of the movie *An American in Paris (1951)* with Gene Kelly. Having grown up in Los Angeles, I'd been raised by the movies. As the only son and youngest child of my parents, I was a lonely kid, and the movies were the place I went to escape. Making my own way around LA on my bike, I went to revival houses, big old cinema houses, or any hole in the wall where I could see flickering images, hear the clicking of a projector and smell fresh buttery popcorn. I even found places that showed silent films on Wednesdays with someone banging away on an ancient piano to accompany it. The movies taught me just about everything I knew about the world. And now, Gene Kelly was entering my mind, calming me with his graceful dancing across milk-splattered streets meant to look like Paris.

The old man took me by the arm, and we walked toward the *sortie*, shuffling together like *two* old men. I was just forty, but at that moment was feeling more like eighty. Paris had defeated me already, upon my *arrival*. Taking it slow, maybe I could start again.

Sortie. It was all over the place. I'd been staring at the exit signs for well over an hour without any comprehension. Perhaps I should have learnt THIS useful word for my first ever trip to Paris. Katie must have assumed I knew it. She'd lived in the UK all her life and her ear had become used to French. Paris was not a foreign place to *her*. But to an American, Paris is half a world away. As foreign as China.

Katie and I lived in the tiny town of St. Ives, in Cornwall, where I first met her. Our daughter, Ariel, was now seven. St. Ives is a peaceful little corner of England, where nothing much happens, and we like it that way. But my boss, Leslie Stringer, told me she'd had just about enough of my nice quiet photographs of Cornwall. She wanted me to go to Paris and jazz up my photographs with a bit of glamour, a bit of depth. She got me a grant and was sending me to Paris to discover something new with my camera. She wanted me to 'grow as an artist' and was sure a month spent in Paris taking pictures of whatever interested me would do the trick. 'All the great fashion and street photographers do it. You'll come back with fresh eyes!' And her eyes were glowing when she said it. I knew Leslie was a big fan of Paris. She had a flat she kept there for her 'get away' trips. 'I'd rather live in Cornwall and escape to Paris

7

rather than the other way around,' she told me. I guess she thought this would be good for me too. And since there was grant money for me to go, why not? Leslie was going to feature my pictures in the next edition of *Cornwall Now*, a rather daring move on her part. 'You know, country mouse, city mouse kind of thing. What the country mouse sees in the city.' I took slight offense at this, I was from Los Angeles after all, not Cornwall. But she was the boss and I'd go along with her grand experiment. I was being paid to and, I considered her a friend. I knew she was trying to help me be a better photographer, expand my ways of seeing.

Leslie showed me her books about the great photographers of the Paris of the 1950s – guys like Robert Doisneau, the one who took those unforgettable black and white pictures of couples kissing. You know the ones. Even in America, I knew them. And there was Henri Cartier-Bresson, who caught those empty Paris streets with all their twists and turns, kids carrying wine bottles, and old men reading newspapers. He took pictures of models too, in the streets, and policemen and scenes with people from all walks of life.

Years ago, when I was an art and photography teacher back in California, I taught my students about these photographers. They were among the many great ones I admired. They were *artists*, but I wasn't sure I was one. So, what was I going to do now? Here in Paris? I had no idea how to make art or where to find the things she wanted me to take pictures of. Leslie had given me a blank canvas and the keys to her flat in Paris. Now I'd lost those keys, had no money or passport, and no idea what to do next.

When we came up all those stairs into the sunlight, I had to shield my eyes, the brightness was so startling. The old man was holding on to my elbow and leading me up the stairs like I was on crutches. I did have a crippling ignorance of Paris. His helping me was an act of pure kindness. *Well, maybe*, said my cynical side. *There's nothing left to steal.* My hands went to the two cameras around my neck. *Oh yes, there was.*

We came to a bench, and he offered it to me with his extended hand. *Good manners.* This man, looking every bit like a vagrant, carried himself like a king. He was in no rush and had complete command of himself and his surroundings. He knew the rules here. I did not. This moment of pause was welcome. I sat down and then he sat beside me. He clasped his hands over his belly, while I held tight to my cameras, and together we watched people emerge from the train station. But just having the sun on my cheeks and some fresh air was helping. I badly needed this rest, and he seemed content to stay here with me and take one too.

After some time had passed, he turned to me and said, 'Where to go?'

I had to think. *Sketchbook. The address of Leslie's flat was written there.* Unzipping my backpack, I pulled out a little black book and flipped through the pages until I found it.

'Rue St Martin.'

'Ah!' His face lit up in wonder as he pointed to the road. 'Here!'

'This street?' I could hardly believe it. Was it just dumb luck that we had come out this sortie from the Gare du Nord to the road I was looking for? Leslie said it was easy to find from the station. If I could just get to the flat and knock on the communal door, perhaps the landlady would have pity on me and let me in. My newly formed cynical side, however, was on high alert. Perhaps the old man wanted to come along because he expected a reward of some kind. Or perhaps, he was going to take me down some side street, hit me on the head and take my cameras. I was clearly too weak to fight him.

'Let's go. I walk you,' he said, as he stood up and smiled at me.

My face became a mask of fear, and he saw it. The pity came back to his eyes. I must have looked like a pathetic

American tourist, afraid of everything. He sighed heavily and took a step back as if to give me room to collect myself.

'It's OK,' I said, my hands out, fingers splayed, like I was trying to calm *him* down. 'Thanks for your help. I'll be fine now. I'll find it myself, thank you.' Standing up, I waved like a lunatic, hoping he would take the hint and leave, but he just stood there with searching eyes.

'Coffee?' he asked, pointed across the street to a little café.

I wanted one badly, but I shrugged my shoulders and did a bad imitation of a tramp with empty pockets. *No money.*

He pulled me by the arm and touched his chest. *He* was going to buy *me* a coffee. This was unexpected and somewhat humiliating, but at the time I wanted a coffee more than anything and didn't protest. For the second time that day, this man rescued me. We shuffled across the road.

When we were inside the little cafe, he drew me to a table and sat me down. Releasing my backpack and suitcase to the floor, I clutched the two cameras around my neck. With wide eyes I took in my surroundings. A Paris café. Elegant. Intimate. The walls a pale shade of green, like a new leaf. There were black and white photographs in dark wood frames. The Eiffel Tower. The Seine. Lovers holding hands.

Glasses tinkled. There was laughter. Voices all around me were speaking French, effortlessly. The sound was a river of words passing by me. Incomprehensible. Pleasant. A babbling brook. The cafe had the same chairs and tables in every movie I'd ever seen about Paris. Woven rattan with a familiar pattern.

A waiter stopped in front of us, dressed in black with a long white apron wrapped around his slender physique. His face was a smooth, hard surface. The expression one of coolness as he took us in, an incongruous pairing of a Paris vagabond and an American tourist. My savior spoke. I understood that at least, two coffees. The waiter took the order with a nod of his head. Then disappeared.

The old man smiled again, raised his shoulders, and then dropped them. We couldn't very well have a conversation. But it seemed polite to try.

'Me Grant,' I said, pointing to myself like I was *Tarzan*. Then I pointed my finger at him.

'Maurice,' he said, and bowed. Clearly *not* an ape man.

Then it suddenly came back to me, the one word I should have known.

'Bonjour!'

He laughed and nodded, like the proud parent of a toddler.

'Oui! Bonjour!

Then another word rose to the tip of my brain.

'Merci! Merci, Maurice! Merci!'

And that was it. Every word I knew in French. I had nothing more. We both stared at our hands for a while and then looked around the café. Other diners looked away when I caught them staring. We were both unwelcome guests here, but it didn't seem to bother Maurice as much as it did me.

I was relieved when the coffee came, along with two little packets of what I'd been trained of late to call 'biscuits' but what in America I'd called 'cookies.' I poured milk and sugar into my cup. My sweet tooth was possibly the only part of me that was excited to be in Paris. Patisseries! That's where I'd find pastries. Heavenly ones, so I'd been told. The coffee hit me like the drug it was and suddenly my brain got busy. *'Shouldn't you be making a call to your bank?'*

I tried to tell the fear in me to relax. First things first. Coffee. Then I would thank the man and drag my suitcase down the long street of Rue St Martin until I found number 290. I'd throw myself on the mercy of the lady in charge of the flats. She would be expecting me. Leslie had arranged it all. Her name was...was...oh, oh, I didn't even have a swear word in French. I had it written in the book somewhere. I'd find it.

While my mind tried to form a plan, Maurice was enjoying his coffee. It was as refreshing him, as it was to me. He sat a little taller in his seat and smiled as he studied the pictures on the walls. I confess, I worried again that he might follow me, and wondered how to politely get him to leave me alone.

'You live near here?' I asked, as if I was going to visit him soon.

He laughed.

'No.' Then, as if trying to turn it into a lesson, he added, 'Non.'

I nodded and repeated. 'Non.' Lesson received. We both sipped our coffee. After some time, the waiter came over and set the bill on the table in front of me. He waited, his eyes meeting mine. I turned to Maurice who put his hand in his pocket and pulled out some coins, laying them on the table. The waiter collected them and gave a small nod to Maurice. To me it was a clear sign that we were to leave the premises. I finished my cup of coffee and set it down but noticed that Maurice took his time. He'd paid for this spot, and he was going to enjoy it. Just as I was wondering where he laid his head at night, he stood up and pointed to somewhere in the back.

'Toilette,' he said. I understood that one with no trouble. Another French word I knew without knowing it!

Maybe I'd be all right after all. I nodded and he disappeared for ten minutes. He was probably having a bath in the sink. Much as I wanted to do the same, I was determined to wait until I had a toilette of my own in the flat that awaited me. I was not prepared to leave my things with this man while I went down the hall into who knew what.

When he returned, looking refreshed, I stood up. We went outside together. I stopped at the pavement and held out my big American hand.

'Merci,' I said again, knowing full well my pronunciation was miserable, but at least it was the right word.

The man looked surprised, and then a little hurt.

'You go now?' he asked.

'Oui!' I was getting the hang of this. 'Merci! Merci!' I smiled. I waved.

'You OK?'

'Oui! Merci!'

He patted my arm, leaving his hand there longer than was strictly necessary. Another kind of fear entered my head. Maybe Maurice expected a little something more in the way of a *reward*. But no. He backed away and smiled a weary smile and then headed back to the train station. I watched him go, a little ashamed of the relief I felt in his going.

When he was out of sight, I turned around and marched down the street, turning my head left and right to try to spot numbers on the buildings. After several minutes of this I was confident I was going the right way. It wasn't exactly close, but I carried on. The bag and backpack were feeling heavier and heavier with each step. Why was I so tired? It couldn't be jet lag. The flight had only been two hours. Of course, it had been about eight hours now since I'd landed and taken the train to Paris from the airport. I wanted to call Katie but thought perhaps I should wait until things were looking a little better.

When I finally found the door, my shoulders drooped. It looked like a fortress! The doors were so *big*. And by now I felt like Dorothy, having just arrived at the doors to the Emerald City. I rang the bell, with hope, and waited. Nothing. I rang it again. Still nothing. Finally, there was a tinny sound of a voice crackling on a wire.

'Oui!'

'Ah! Hello! I mean, Bonjour. I'm Grant Decker. You are expecting me? The American? The friend of Leslie Stringer? I'm afraid I've lost my keys. Do you speak English?'

A loud buzz. Giving the door a push with my shoulder, it opened.

I heard a distant slapping sound which grew louder. Footsteps approached me, coming down a spiral staircase,

16

echoing on the walls. Waiting patiently at the foot of the stairs, I ran my hand through my hair, which must have been a mess after all I'd been through. My hair tends to have a mind of its own.

The first thing I saw was the long skirt. Then, worn shoes. A long apron. The woman looked like an extra from the set of *Les Misérables*. Her arms were crossed, and she stood on the third step, towering above me, with disdain.

'Vous ne parlez pas français?'

My brain turned around three times and then went to sleep.

'Non.' Then again. 'Merci.' Oops. I just said thank you. 'I mean, sorry. Very sorry.'

'American.' She spoke the word like a curse.

'Oui.' I was hoping she was impressed, even just a little, that I'd made it.

'Grant Decker. Leslie's friend.'

She closed her eyes a moment, as if counting to ten, and then blinked them open.

'Your passport.' She took two more steps and extended her hand.

'I was robbed, Madame ... Madame...' I strained to remember what Leslie said her name was. 'Madame Garnier. They got my passport, my keys, my bankcards, my money.'

Her shaggy eyebrows came together in consternation.

'But I had the address. Leslie Stringer sent me?'

I fumbled in my backpack and pulled out the sketchbook, found the address and held it out for her to scrutinize.

She took a deep breath and then her mouth settled into a scowl.

After turning around, she started up the stairs again. One foot, whack. The next foot, whack. A clawing hand gripped the dull wood railing. She stopped and looked back over her shoulder at me.

'Come!' she boomed.

I snapped to attention, slung my backpack over my shoulder, picked up my bag and mounted the squeaky stairs behind her. For what seemed like ten minutes we climbed them together like mountaineers tethered to one another. It was three floors, a lot of steps. She stopped and unlocked the door marked with the number seven.

After ushering me in, she threw the keys on a table in the room. A quick survey showed a single bed next to an entire wall of books. That was Leslie for you. An avid reader.

'You make new keys.'

'Where?'

'Train station.'

'Oh. All right. Yes.'

She took a step closer and put her enormous finger in my face.

'You report to Police!'

I blinked.

'Police?'

'The robbery! You tell police.'

'What? Oh no, no, no, that's all right. No need.' We didn't report crimes in LA. I tried once, but the officer on the other end of the phone just laughed.

Mrs. Garnier stiffened. Her eyes wide open.

'You must! Tomorrow. Police.'

Right. OK. This is what they do in Paris!

'Oui, Madame.'

She nodded and seemed satisfied.

'You get more money?'

'Oui. I'll call my bank now.'

I smiled, trying to appear confident and capable.

She rolled her eyes, shrugged, pointed to the laminated piece of paper with the WIFI code on it. Then turned to leave me to it, slamming the door behind her.

I dropped my bag and backpack to the floor and collapsed into the one padded chair. My muscles unclenched for the first time in hours. How long had I been like this? I pulled the code closer and entered it into my phone. The time changed. Was it just three in the afternoon here? It seemed like I'd left the UK weeks ago. I sighed. Oh well. At least I had a roof over my head now and was in a *compound*. Well protected. *Thank you, Leslie.*

After some minutes of silent prayer and meditation, I found the international emergency number from the back of my bankcard. To my astonishment someone answered.

'Hello? You've reached the Lost or Stolen number at HSBC. I'm Ron. Who am I speaking with?'

'Grant Decker. This is HSBC?'

'Yes, indeed, Mr. Decker. Are you calling to report your card lost or stolen?'

'Uh ... yes...'

We went through all the security questions, and I had all the answers written on my little bit of paper.

'I'm so sorry this happened to you.' He said it gently, like he might be speaking to someone mad or dangerous. 'Now, was it lost or stolen?'

'Stolen. Pickpocketed. Right when I arrived in Paris.'

'Oh, that's the worst. Happened to me too. Awful. I'm so sorry. You weren't injured, were you?'

The concern had escalated.

'No. I'm fine.'

'Well, that's a relief! And that's what's most important. Sorry to say, pickpocketing is a terrible problem here. So many unsuspecting tourists, you see. Did you know over

4,000 tourists lose their wallets and passports to pickpockets in Paris every month?'

'What?'

'Astonishing, isn't it? So, you're not alone. Did they get your passport too?'

'They did. How did you know?'

'These are professionals, Mr. Decker. They work in groups. It was several people who robbed you. A gang. Not just one. Anyway, don't you worry about a thing. I'm here to help. We're going to take care of all of it. First things first. Your bank card was taken. Correct?'

'Yes. And you can call me Grant.'

'Thank you, Grant. And please, you call me Ron. I'm going to get a new card out to you right away. What is your address in Paris and how long are you staying?'

'Oh, I'll be here for four weeks.' I gave him the address. 'How long will it take to get the new card?'

'I will expedite it. You should have it in three days. If you go to the nearest bank which is, one moment...on the Champs-Élysées, I'll arrange to have some euros there to tide you over until the card comes. Can you find the branch there, Grant?'

I liked that he called me Grant. Every time he said my name, I felt comforted. Like he was a new friend.

'Yes. I can find it. I still have my map of Paris.'

'Shall I have 2000 euros there for you? That's 1,680 pounds and 47 pence.'

'Crikey!' I loved any excuse to use that British expression. 'Do I need that much?'

'It's Paris.'

'Hmmm. How much do you think I'll need for four weeks?'

'Oh, that all depends entirely on how much fun you plan on having, doesn't it?' He chuckled. 'Up to you, of course, but you want enough cash to get through your time without a card and maybe some more if you want to avoid fees for getting cash out of a machine. Do you have somewhere safe to keep money where you're staying? You don't want to carry too much around on your person while you're out.'

'Right.' I was beginning to understand there was a lot to learn about moving around Paris safely.

Ron explained how to buy a metro ticket. He knew exactly where the key maker was at the station. He was incredibly helpful. On *my* team. He took a long time with me on the phone. Like he had no other customers in the world right now but me.

'Now the next thing to do after you have money is to go to the US Embassy. As you might imagine, there are a lot of other Americans in your situation, trying to get a new passport. But don't worry. They'll do it. Same day.'

'Same day passport? Really?'

'It's the least they can do.'

'Well ... I'm ... impressed.'

'You can rest easy now. Once you have your metro pass for a month, pick up your cash, get a new passport, duplicate your keys, you'll be right as rain. The card will be with you in three days. Is there anything else I can help you with, Grant?'

'No, I ... no, I think that's everything. Thank you, Ron. Thank you so much.'

'Oh, that's what I'm here for, Grant. I've got you. If anything else occurs to you, just call me back, all right? My personal extension number is 3777. Got it?'

'Got it.'

'I'm here for you.'

'Gosh.'

'Au revoir, Grant.'

'Thank you, Ron. Merci!'

'Oh, very good! That's the spirit! Don't let this get you down. Paris is wonderful, you'll see. This was just a little setback. But we got it sorted for you. Now, if I may offer a little free advice?'

'Go on.'

'Put your keys and wallet in a VERY secure place on your person. Pocket in FRONT of you. With another layer of clothing over it. NEVER, EVER have your backpack on your *back*. You can't see the zippers from there. If you MUST have a backpack, wear it in front of you. Keep your wallet where only you can get to it. Understand?'

'Yes, yes. Thank you. I'll do as you say.'

'Just have to do things a little differently in Paris. That's all. You'll learn. It's part of the adventure of travel!'

Katie would say that too. I liked this guy. He was right. I had to get over this fear now of being robbed. I just had to learn new routines.

'Right. I'm going to be fine.'

'Sure, you will. Ride the subways, just for practice. They take some getting used to. Best of luck now. Goodbye, Grant.'

And he hung up.

What a nice guy!

For the first time ever, I loved my bank. *This* was great service when I really needed it. Everything was fixed. I could call Katie now and not feel pathetic.

I dialed our home number.

Chapter Two

'Hi, honey! Bonjour!'

'Grant! Are you OK? I was a bit worried.'

'Sorry honey, there was just a ... a delay... I got a bit lost, but I finally found the flat and I'm here now.'

'Good. Are you tired out?'

'Yeah. How're you? How's Ariel?'

'We're fine.'

'And Cassandra?' I cringed. *Mistake!*

'Boy, you must be tired! She's hissing at me right now. She knows it's you.'

'Yeah. Good old Cassandra.' The cat who hated my guts.

'Grant? Something's not right. I can hear it in your voice. What happened?'

I sighed. There was no fooling Katie.

'Well, oh, it's just embarrassing, that's all.'

'It's upset you. Tell me.'

I blinked back tears. Manly tears. And did the manly squeezing of my eyes thing with my fingers.

'I was robbed.'

'What? Oh honey! When? How?'

I let out a long breath.

'Pickpocketed on the train. By a gang of thieves, apparently. Professionals. You know, it happens to over 4,000 tourists every month here! Can you believe it? Every month!'

'That's astonishing. What did they get?'

'Oh, everything. Wallet. Passport. Keys.'

She gasped. 'Sweetheart! My poor baby! Where are you? Were you hurt?'

'No. I'm fine. The landlady let me into the flat. But you know what? Writing down the emergency lost or stolen number and all the security details for my bank really paid off. They fixed everything. I had the information in a separate pocket.'

'Good *thinking*.'

'Yeah. Ron is sending me a new card. He'll have euros for me at the bank tomorrow. He told me how to get a metro card and everything. I'm all set. He was so nice.'

'Ron? You're on a first name basis with the guy at a call center?'

'It's a special number of the bank. For victims of loss or theft. I was in good hands. These guys must be specially trained. Like grief counselors.'

'Wow. Who knew? That's impressive. What about your passport?'

'He said I can go the embassy and get it the same day!'

'The same *day*?'

'I know. Hard to believe, eh? But with that many Americans losing their passports every day, they've gotta speed it up somehow. It can't be too hard to print out another one.'

'I guess.'

'It's the least they can do.'

My wife laughed at this.

'Right.'

'It's true!'

'If you say so. And your keys?'

'I'm getting copies made for the flat tomorrow, after the other things.'

'Will you have to change the locks?'

'No. The address was in my sketchbook, and they didn't take that. So, the thieves have no way of knowing which flat the keys are for. They aren't marked in any way. I'll just get a copy made. And this place is a *fortress*. Big heavy double doors and about nine other flats facing a courtyard in the middle. You can see your neighbors.'

'Nice. Then you can all look out for each other.'

'Yeah, I'll be just fine. So, let's talk about you. How was work?'

'Oh, the usual. Nothing too stressful.'

'And the surfing today?'

'Beautiful, but not as many waves as I like. I'm just enjoying being in the water this time of year.'

'Well, you be careful. You know how July can be.'

'I'll be fine. YOU be careful. Are you sure you're going to be all right? Paris can be a rough place.'

'Non, Merci. I'll be fine.'

She laughed at my worldliness, which had, amazingly enough, returned to me.

'I see you have the language well in hand.'

'Honey, I'm so sorry I didn't study your list, but I'm motivated now. It's a real pain if you can't speak the language.'

'Oui. Well, I'm glad you're sorted. Well done. Love you, dear.'

'You too, *ma Chéri*. I'll check in again in a few days. I'm not exactly sure what I'm doing, but I suppose I'll figure it out in time.'

'You will. Just use your eyes. You're a photographer.'

'Thanks, my love. Au revoir.'

Having mangled French enough for one day, I hung up.

My confidence was gaining momentum now. I took my time exploring my new little flat. Leslie called it her 'bolt hole,' her hideaway. She loved Paris and spoke fluent French. Half the books on her bookshelves were in French. I was so impressed. Opening a few, I saw the language was even more frightening on the page than it was to my ear.

The flat was basically one big room with low ceilings and exposed wooden beams. The tall windows that faced the courtyard had wood shutters on them for privacy, but you could push them back and open the windows like doors. Most people had their windows open because it was hot. Oppressively so. And there was no air conditioning, either.

With the windows open you could hear the lives of others spilling from the windows. Creaking floors. Crying babies. The distant hum of traffic, a background noise that never seemed to stop. Cats meowed. A dog barked. I looked over the windowsill to see two children playing ball down there in the courtyard. School was obviously over for the day. The smoke from a cigarette wafted across the hot afternoon and snaked into my window. Looking up across the courtyard to the next story I saw a window open with a hunchbacked old lady staring down at me. Our eyes met. She took another drag on her cigarette and blew smoke at me. I turned and moved further inside to the privacy of my new little home.

Shadows slowly crept across the courtyard, as I studied my map of Paris. The city was divided into 'arrondissements,' which were basically sections of the city radiating outward and numbered according to how close you were to the center. My flat was in the 4th arrondissement. I could walk to the river from here easily and find places like the Louvre. I figured it would be about a forty-minute walk to the bank tomorrow in the Champs-Élysées. No problem. The US Embassy was close to the bank. I'd just go right over there too. And I supposed, if I had time, I could stop in at a police station and report the crime, just to please Madame Garnier. The keys I could get on the way back.

My nose twitched. Onions and garlic sizzled on someone's stove. I sat down in the chair at the table and picked up my camera and focused on the windows of my neighbor. Snap, snap, snap. The sound was soothing. Familiar. It felt a little like spying, but it always felt that way. Part of the job. Observe life. Capture it. I imagined the neighbors already knew about me. Madame Garnier had probably spread the word about the American who arrived for a month, with no keys, no passport, and no wallet. The clock on the wall said five thirty. I was getting hungry. My stomach growled. No lunch! I stood up. It was time to feed.

I realized however that I had no money to go out and buy things. The little kitchen along the back wall had a tiny red fridge. Inside, I was thrilled to see a small glass bottle of milk. On the counter was a basket with a fresh baguette inside. Two apples were in there too, and some cheese wrapped in wax paper. Madame Garnier wasn't as mean as she looked.

Classical music drifted through the air into my window, adding a touch of class to the neighborhood. An announcer's voice, speaking in French, of course, confirmed that it came from a radio. A woman sang gently with the melody, as if she were alone, unselfconsciously. I sliced my bread and cheese as I listened, enchanted by the intimacy of this singing, the sweetness of the voice.

I sat down at my little table with a cheese sandwich and an apple and felt the wonder of it all. My new home. My new life. In Paris. It was happening. The plans made real. As I poured the cold milk into my empty glass there was a satisfying sound that reminded me of plentitude. I had everything I needed for the moment.

This chair must have been where Leslie sat when she was here, listening to these sounds, eating bread and cheese like this. It was strange to think of her in this French life, as

31

if she were another person entirely, one I did not know. My boss, who ran a magazine about Cornwall from St. Ives, must have slipped into a whole other part of herself when she came here. Would I find another part of me too?

After placing the dishes in the sink, I wandered over to the bookshelf. There were a *lot* of books by and about Ernest Hemingway. I could almost hear the waves slapping against the boat. Now, I picked out a biography of Hemingway and stared at the photo on the cover. There he was. The man with the grey beard, the cable knit sweater and the *glare*. It was a good photo. Every detail crisp and sharp. The contrast showing the texture. The patterns of his beard similar yet different to the sweater. In black and white it felt symbolic of Hemingway, a no-nonsense writer who wrote in simple language. Every word was powerful and essential. These photographers had a job to do, like I had a job to do. Take a picture of this or that. But they were thinking hard about composition, symbolism, the position of the subject, the light. They were composing a visual language and saying something *about* Hemingway with it. Maybe what I'd been doing with my pictures of Cornwall was more subconscious. I was responding to beauty. But was I putting into practice the things I'd tried to teach my students? I could analyze photos, but could I make them? Maybe Leslie's purpose in sending me here was to have me observe artists and the city that inspired them. I might find a similar spark in myself, a similar urge to create, compose and say something with my photos. Settling down on the bed, I switched on the reading light and began.

I don't know how many hours passed, but when I looked up there were lights on across the yard, dotting the windows like stars in the darkness. The noises were winding down. It was getting late, and I decided it was time for me to try and sleep. My eyelids were heavy. I didn't bother getting undressed. Snapping off the light, I slipped into sleep.

Chapter Three

The next morning the sun poured through the open windows, piercing the chill of the night. I threw off the bedsheet. There were the sounds and smells of a new day. Coffee. Toast. Tantrums. Phones ringing. Radio blaring. The news was in French. Why does news sound the same in any language? Serious and depressing. I heard arguments, the unmistakable sound of family discord. Crabbiness at close quarters. A dog barked. A man yelled at it. Walking to the window I saw a cat making its way along a narrow external windowsill and my heart lurched. Would it fall? No. Cats in all places know exactly what they are doing. I thought of

Cassandra, the fat old tabby we inherited from Katie's mother. She hated me with a disdain that bordered on passion. It was her only activity, hating me. Surely, she missed me. I missed my own little family this morning. Even Cassandra, who was, without a doubt, part of it.

The smell of toast and coffee made me hungry, so I tore off the last crust of bread and cut the last of the cheese into slices. Ariel always had the same thing for breakfast: porridge oats with raisins, cinnamon, and milk. Katie had yogurt with fruit of the season. Right now, it would be the last of the British strawberries. I liked eggs, over easy, with a bagel, toasted and buttered with a little jam.

Katie would be dropping Ariel at school about now and then go into her law office above the bookstore. How British school children managed to endure school until the end of July was beyond me, but at least they didn't have to go back until mid-September. I missed reading to Ariel at bedtime and playing our favorite game. She straightened her back and started it off.

'I am from Poland, but I lived in France. I mixed chemicals together and helped people in a terrible war. My Name Is?'

'What chemicals?'

Eye roll.

'You're stalling...'

'Male or female?'

'I gave you three clues!'

'It's on the tip of my tongue.'

'You don't know it. I win.'

'Do you know it?'

'Madame Curie.'

'Of course! Foiled again.'

'Your turn.'

And so it would go. A seven-year-old with a serious interest in history, beating me at this game roundly. It seemed I was always catching up to what my daughter was learning. What would she know by the time I got back?

I finished the last apple and the milk. I'd have my first coffee of the day once I came out of the bank with my money. So, this would have to do.

How could Katie let me go on this trip? We'd never been apart this long before. How did she think I could manage by myself for four whole weeks? Well. It's true that I'd handled the robbery all right on my own. Maybe it wouldn't be so bad. It wasn't like I was far away. I was just over the channel, after all. Things were *basically* the same here, weren't they? They had banks, the metro, taxis, just like in the UK. I'd be fine. At least they didn't eat bees here, like in China! Well, they ate snails. I closed my eyes. I missed Katie.

After a shower in the tiny, closet-size bathroom, I got dressed. Then I laid out my keys and map on the table and stared at them. Right. It was time. My first day in Paris. Traveling *light,* I decided not to even take my cameras. Not yet. Today was about getting to know the place a little. Finding my feet. The keys were going in my front jeans pocket where I could *always feel them.* My short-sleeved shirt had a front pocket and that was where I would put my little map and the new passport. The new metro card would go there too. Luckily, I'd packed my cargo pants with other pockets in the front where I could put a new wallet. For today, this would do.

I wanted to ride the metro and learn the layout of the city before I started taking pictures. In a few days, I'd figure out how to move around with my cameras, but for now, I didn't want to distract myself with worry. I wanted to travel light and keep my eyes open. Understand the layout of Paris. I took a deep breath and let it out. I was going to stay alert. Going out the door to my flat, I locked it and went down the stairs. Every squeaky one.

Madame Garnier was standing by the huge front door with a mop, her hair pushed back with a bright blue scarf tied up in a knot above her forehead.

'Bonjour, Madame Garnier,' I said and smiled. It sounded almost right.

Her eyelids were half closed but those black eyes were trained on me.

'You go police?'

'Oui, Madame. Right after the bank and the embassy.'

She nodded and stuck the mop into a bucket of grey water.

I went out the door. It closed behind me with a loud thunk and locked automatically. The hairs on my arm stood up. *I'm on my own. In Paris.* I touched the keys in my font pocket. Yes, there were two. The front door and my flat door. Before me was a river of people and I started moving my legs to join the stream. It was already warm, the sun beating down on my head, but I didn't mind. It felt nice to be alive and well in Paris. Everyone moved down the street with purpose.

There was the sound of jackhammers, the ring and clash of heavy metal things being dropped on the street. Scaffolding was going up. Cement mixers were whirring. Cranes groaning. Motors straining. It looked like an archaeological excavation was going on, everywhere. Old walls could be seen under newer walls. Buckets of stones were being hauled away. Paris began on the tiny island of Île de la Cité by Celt fishermen in 259 BC. I was surprised to learn that on my phone. The idea that Paris was started by a Celt must have annoyed the French. But it grew from there.

Spreading outward. How anyone managed to build here, I could not imagine. It was layers and layers of history. But it was also *alive* with continuous activity, the *new* surging into existence on top of and alongside the past.

There were cars honking, cyclists ringing their bells, people shouting. I tried to feel confident, but already I was in despair. Where were the street signs? I didn't see any.

I kept moving toward the bigger, wider streets. Surely, they would lead me to the Seine. That's what I was counting on. I didn't pull out my map until I was standing off to the side, by a little strip of green grass and an oblong painted metal cabinet. It was probably constructed to cover telephone equipment of some kind or an electrical box. As I studied the map for some landmarks, I heard the sudden gushing of water and the wall of the metal box behind me moved! I jumped away as a door slid open and a man walked out, as surprised to see me standing there as I was to see him. He shouted something at me, probably something like, 'Out of my way American!' Then he waved his hand as he moved into the flood of walkers on the pavement.

When he was gone, I noticed the door sliding back, leaving the metal circle as it was before. It dawned on me that this was a public convenience. A loo! I'd seen something like it in London. They were painted green and had the unmistakable fussy details of Victorian architecture. This, however, was a sly modern sculpture that looked quite at home in the cityscape. As I walked around it, I finally saw the little slits for the coins. That reminded me. I needed money, even for a loo, so it was back to the mission. The bank. But first I took a moment to pause. Behind me there was a building from the 19ᵗʰ century. Beyond *that*, was the river Seine.

It looked calm. Muddy but peaceful. The morning light sparkled on it like gems floating on the surface. For a very long time the Seine had meandered through Paris, a steady presence in its long and turbulent history. I was standing before a bridge that went to one of the two islands that the Seine flowed around: Île de la Citié and Île Saint-Louis. It was tempting to walk across the bridge on this beautiful morning and explore these islands, the birthplace of Paris. But I had to stick to the plan. Turn right at the bridge and walk along the Seine. By the Jardin des Tuileries. To the Place de la Concorde and then left. The sooner I got my cash, the sooner I'd have my coffee and ... yes. I was getting a real *croissant*. In *Paris*.

One foot in front of the other, I marched on. I took the steps down to the path to the stonewall, directly beside the river. Trees offered shade, standing in orderly rows, springing up from little openings in the grey dirt. The furious noise of the road – the taxis, the trucks, the bikes, reached me from above. Only the river was my companion and the sound of my own footsteps. An occasional barge or houseboat floated by. Then a boat carrying tourists. A tugboat. In that moment it reminded me of the Thames. A working river.

I passed many more bridges, individual men fishing, with their poles and tackle boxes. More houseboats. Residences tied up to the moorings, plants carefully attended, laundry out on a line. There were young people walking. Children. Old people. Couples holding hands. Dogs.

I passed the Arc de Triomphe and imagined Hitler there. The photographs were part of our collective consciousness now. Everyone must have seen them somewhere. How horrible that must have been. The man hated by everybody on French soil, taking it all in like he was on a holiday, destroying people's lives, homes, and histories. My hands were shaking. Time for a coffee.

When I finally walked through the doors of my bank, I'll admit it was a relief to hear English, even if it was English English. It didn't take nearly as much effort to understand what was being said. *Here,* they had sympathy. They understood how I felt. The man passed me my money. 'Stiff upper lip,' he seemed to be saying with his smile. I took the euros and stuffed them into my other front jeans pocket.

Then I gave the man my friendliest American wave, which meant, 'No hard feelings, Englishman. We've got a 'special' relationship, thanks to World War II. Thanks for the help.'

Not too surprisingly, there was a patisserie near the bank. It served wonderful coffee and real, flaky, warm *French* croissants. I had three. I simply could not believe my taste buds. Not the first or second time. These croissants had little resemblance to the dry, lifeless things we had back in England. The flavors lingered in my mouth, melted on my tongue. And the bakery had many other delightful-looking things. Too many for my tired brain to comprehend. I felt like, well, a *foreigner* to the world of patisseries. If I was going to explore Paris, I was going to have to walk a great deal doing it or I'd become very fat tasting all these amazing treats.

One thing I noticed sitting there outside, at my little table on the Champs-Élysées, was how many supermodels were walking around. A model, to my mind, is a beautiful woman. A supermodel is one that looks like you should know her face because she's been on so many billboards or magazines that she's become famous. This place was full of them. I don't look at fashion magazines so I couldn't tell you exactly who they were, but even in my limited experience of that world, they looked familiar.

Incredibly beautiful, very thin, these women wandered about in small groups like gazelles chatting away in French. They had designer name shopping bags on their arms and wore skimpy dresses that left little to the imagination. Dazzling mixtures of scents swirled in the air as they passed. Exotic and intoxicating. After a while, I put two and two together. Here were the banks and shops with names like Louis Vuitton, Cartier, Tiffany and Co. I suppose this was what Leslie was talking about when she said to find the glamour in Paris. She was the glamorous type. Leslie didn't have to work. She loved art and photography and was bankrolling this magazine as an attempt to draw more rich people to Cornwall for their holidays. It was an attempt to support the tourist industry. These must have been the people she had in mind. Champs-Élysées folk. The people of the Elysian fields. A paradise, in Greek mythology. I suppose this was paradise if you were young, rich, and good looking. But the square trees here, planted in orderly rows, were not my idea of a paradise. In fact, they put me off. I didn't have any impulses to take pictures in this place.

If I had any magic at all as a photographer, then I had to have two things to work with. One was my camera, my partner in the desire to make art. And the other was the impulse to take a shot. Cornwall had no end of beauty. The coastline was glorious, varied, and interesting. The hills and farms, the strange man-made stones carefully arranged, from thousands of years ago. The animals. The people. The birds. I never got tired of looking at Cornwall. Which is why I felt lucky to live there and to have the job of taking pictures of it. But I could understand and appreciate how seeing a different place might also present a different way to see.

Now I watched people walk by me for a while longer. This was Paris to some people. But I didn't feel that instinct yet to capture it with a camera. Just as well I'd left both at the flat. Checking my cup, I realized the last of the coffee was gone. I stood up to go. Well, today was not my day to take pictures anyway. There was still much of Paris to see, and I had to have faith that there would be something that stirred me.

Helpfully, the bank people had circled the Embassy on my map and advised me to set my sights on it, after a proper coffee, of course. Now that I was refreshed, I had only to find my way to the place where they would speak *American* English. I was looking forward to that. I stroked my chin. The light beard I was planning to grow while in Paris already had a day's start and I imagined I looked a bit swarthy, like Hemingway. Not that the models noticed. I started walking.

It was only about ten minutes later when I came across several roads blocked by police cars. Somewhat alarmed, I approached a French police officer standing in the middle of the road in his sleek blue uniform. I remembered reading somewhere that Pierre Cardin had designed them. It must be true. He looked good. Like a very cool superhero. I stepped up to him and after some hesitation, opened my mouth to speak.

'Where ... is the...'

He held up his gloved hand and his hard blue eyes glared at me. I held my breath. Was I in trouble?

'*First*, we zay ... ello.'

It seemed I was in violation of manners.

'Sorry. Yes. Oui. Bonjour.'

He nodded. Appeased.

'Bonjour.'

'I'm looking for the embassy entrance?' He pointed it out to me. 'Thanks. I got pick-pocketed,' I said, hoping for a sliver of sympathy.

He shrugged.

'It 'appens.'

'Well, uh, thank you, Sir. Uh, Merci.'

We nodded to one another, and I headed for the entrance, where I found a long line. This could take years. It was a good thing I'd had my coffee and croissants, or I would have crumbled in a defeated heap right here. But I took a cleansing breath, stood tall and prepared myself for a long wait. Time passed. I waited. I waited some more, by reviewing the names of all my favorite films, all of Katie's favorite films, all Ariel's favorite films, and every sea shanty I knew. I was missing the boys at the pub. I wouldn't see them for four weeks. When my turn finally came, and I stood at the counter before a man who looked even more bored than I was.

'May I help you?' he said.

'I was pick-pocketed. They got my passport. I'm an American.'

'Any proof of that, Sir?'

I went pale.

'No. They got everything. My wallet. My bank card.'

'No bank card?'

'They're sending me a new one. I just came from my bank.'

'Did they print out a letter to that effect for you?'

'Yes. It's right here.'

I fumbled in my back pocket. I hadn't thought of it as proof of my identity. Where was it! Oh! There it was. I pulled it out and pushed it across the counter to the man with the big nose and purple bags under his eyes.

He leaned forward and examined the letter. It had my name, my home address.

'This says you live in the UK.'

'I do. In Cornwall. But I'm American. You can hear my accent.'

'You have a UK Bank, live in the UK and claim to be an American.'

'That's right. Look, I was robbed. My bank said you deal with this all the time.'

'Yes, we've had forty-six Americans here today, all claiming to have been robbed yesterday and it's only ten o'clock.'

'There'll be more.'

'Yes. There will be.'

'I thought you could look it up or something. I was told I could get a new one today.'

'Who told you that?'

My knees buckled.

Then the man looked me up and down, sighed deeply and gave me a form.

'We will indeed look into your records and if we find you there, we can print out a new one for you.' He pulled up some papers and shoved them across the counter to me.

'What's this?'

'A DS-64. An emergency request for a ten-year passport. We'll take your photo next. If all goes well, you'll have the passport today.'

'Oh! Thank you!'

I took the pen from him and filled it out. He took out a big stamping mechanism and slammed it down on my form.

'Go to window fifty-four.'

'Thank you.'

The relief was enormous. They could have said no since I was living in the UK. Thank God, they believed me. I suppose they had a record of it. I wasn't making it up.

Two hours later, I had my new, ten-year passport in hand. I could hardly believe it. Placing it carefully in my front shirt pocket, I went out the door. *Mission accomplished.* With my new euros, I bought a wallet, at a stand that sold them, conveniently, just outside the embassy. I spotted the same French policeman standing there and, after saying *Bonjour*, I asked him for directions to the police station.

It wasn't far. But no one there spoke English. I was faced with French forms and no help from anyone. Reduced to acting out the pickpocketing, I still got blank stares. This was clearly *my own* little problem. These men were not as interested as Madame Garnier assumed they would be. 'Don't wear your backpack on your back, you fool,' is what they seemed to be saying to me with disdain on their faces, standing there in their cool uniforms. Oh, well. At least I tried.

After I lunched on a ham and cheese croissant at another lovely patisserie, I discovered an entrance to the

Metro. It was in an Art Nouveau style. Enchanting. Well. Croissants make you brave. It was time now to go below ground, to descend into the abyss. There weren't any subways in Cornwall. Going under the pavement felt distinctly wrong to me. Made me twitchy. But I took a deep breath and did it.

The air changed. Ominously. Like the hot breath of the underworld. There were the distant shrieks of trains, whistling and whooshing sounds from tunnels that only helped my mind to conjure demons and devils. But once I got the card from the window of the ticket office, I was all right. I recalled such sights and sounds from the London Underground. The tube map even looked similar. The red line, the green, the blue, the yellow, the purple and brown. I could crisscross the Seine several times, riding the various lines for the whole rest of the day. I wanted to understand how to get around. Knowledge of the scope of this place would help reduce my fear of it. Riding the lines for the day would give me a chance to observe people and places from the window. It was worth my time to get a sense of things.

The La Défense to Chateau Vincennes line had a lot of hotspots. The Louvre, Bastille, Champs-Élysées, Tuileries. It even had a Franklin D. Roosevelt stop! Then there was Porte Dauphine to Nation. And one line made a whole loop around the nineteenth arrondissement. Some of the lines were both above and below ground, and I got to see out the window. By the end of the day, I had a good idea of where everything was and what kind of people were going from point A to point B on the train.

One thing I noticed early on was that I wasn't the only one studying the trains or the people riding them. Every city must have the familiar sight of the down-and-out hanging around public transit. But I saw some on these trains, walking up and down the isles with a cup or empty hat. A few people took out some money and put it in the hat, but most people kept on reading their paper, ignoring them. A few Parisians told them off, shooing them out of the car and expressing their disgust at such behavior. They shook their heads and went back to reading their papers.

There were often performers on the trains too. Offering something of their art for coins. Someone would stand up and start singing an aria or take out a violin and perform. And this changed the atmosphere, an alchemical transformation from being in a steel box waiting to arrive to being at the theater where beauty was happening. Afterward there were polite claps, and a few coins were dropped in a bucket that was passed around. People didn't seem to mind that very much.

In the late afternoon of my roaming there was one extraordinary event. A man wearing a suit of a strange shiny material walked onto the car and found a seat. The look of his suit was unusual. It was a deep green in color. When he moved, the color changed to blue. It certainly attracted stares. Once the doors were closed and the train was at cruising speed, the man got up and stood *on his seat*, bracing himself by holding on to the upper luggage rail. He began to speak in a loud voice as all eyes turned toward him.

He was not drunk or on drugs. He projected his voice in a very professional manner. A story was being told. In French, of course. So, I had no idea what he was saying. At first, I thought it was a sales pitch of some kind, for insurance perhaps. I could not tell what it was, but soon he was showing charts, diagrams, his own drawings. Aliens with big heads. Spaceships. Probes. *Oh, dear.* The man had been abducted and wanted compensation. This was clearly not covered in the French health plan scheme. Amazingly, as he walked down the aisle with his cup, a few people put money in it. The previous scowlers buried their heads in their newspapers again. They had no words for this guy. I stared at his suit. *What made it shine like that?*

The experience was strange, but it had the agreeable effect of making *me* feel less alien. We all got off the car with a bit more energy than we had before. As I continued my journeys to other lines, I watched people's reflection in the windows and studied their faces. By now it became the crowd coming home from work. They didn't notice me watching them as they stared at nothing. These were the faces I wanted to take pictures of. Wishing my camera was with me now, I realized the instinct to snap was returning. *These* faces were marvelous to me because they weren't perfect. Each face was different. In this sea of humanity, a wide range of emotions could be found. In the hours I'd spent riding trains today I'd seen bored, angry, wistful, lonely, and perplexed. There had been stressed people and ones who were sad, dazed, happy, and daydreaming. I'd seen people love. People in pain. The old looking enviously at the young, and the young hungry to be older. It was all here on the trains. And it didn't matter what language they spoke. Their faces were universal. That's what I was here for. To take pictures of *these* faces.

Chapter Four

For someone who had spent the previous day riding trains, I woke up surprisingly sore. Perhaps today, I should do just one thing, not involving trains. Stay closer to home, and just sort of walk about. Go and discover *one* place. A smaller place than the whole of Paris. Take in the ambiance. A little bell went off in my head. *Ambiance. French word.* I was using French now, without thinking about it! Ooh LA LA! Look at *me!* I'd have to tell Katie about that. I pulled the map towards me on the bed.

I was near the Centre Pompidou. An architectural marvel, according to one of the guidebooks on Leslie's shelf. It was the work of Renzo Piano and Richard Rogers. It famously had the 'guts' of the building – the vents, tubes, and escalators, on the outside. Quite controversial, it had become a landmark for art and free thinking. Perfect. I'd go there.

Taking time to shower, dress and look around the room, I carefully came up with a plan for security. Ding ding ding! Securité! That sounded French! Gosh. The language was sprinkled all through English! How did THIS 'appen? I was becoming more conscious of the language. That was a good thing. Right?

My new wallet fitted snuggly in the front pocket of my cargo pants. The two new keys I'd had made at the station were in another front pocket. And today...*today* I was bringing my Nikon D70. I fingered the black leather case and strap, well-worn from hard use. This baby had become my way of earning a living and it was precious to me. Like an old friend. Today, I would use it to explore the place and people at the Centre Pom-pi-dou! But first, I needed breakfast.

As I waited outside the big external door of my flat to join in the river of people on the pavement, my eye caught something across the street. A stand of some kind, not as big as a newspaper stand, but a little bigger than a phone box – it was painted a deep green, and there was a woman inside making something. The smell was wonderful, even from across the street. *Breakfast calling.*

As I approached the green box, the woman smiled. She was maybe in her fifties, with a round face, her hair pulled back and under a bright red scarf. Speaking to me in French, I pleaded ignorance.

'American?' she said. We had a reputation, we ignorant Americans.

'Oui,' I confessed.

Turning to the sign behind her, she pointed. It had pictures of many kinds of crêpes. There were crêpes with bananas, strawberries, blueberries, maple syrup, chocolate, ice-cream. And Nutella! I'd never heard of Nutella until I came to the UK. What a revelation! Hazelnut and chocolate – TOGETHER! In a spread like peanut butter. There were about fifty kinds of crêpes on the board, about half savory and half sweet. I was stumped. Which should I try?

'What's *your* favorite?' I asked.

Without hesitation, she pointed to the crêpe with a picture of a lemon.

'Citron,' she said.

I nodded. A subtle one.

'Citron, s'il vous plaît.' (See-Voo-Play) ← (Handy pronunciation guide)

She got to work, and as I watched, she poured the batter onto the large, round, pizza-sized iron griddle, swirled it around with a wooden stick as if she had done it a thousand times, and we waited for it to cook. While it was doing that, she took a mason jar with sugar and placed it near a paper plate and sliced a lemon in half and then half again. After slipping the crêpe onto the plate, she sprinkled the sugar and squeezed the lemon onto it and handed it to me with shining brown eyes.

The paper plate was warm in my hands. I set it down on the countertop and realized I had only a large bill to give her. I glanced up at the prices. Two euros. I cringed as I passed her the twenty.

'Nothing smaller?' she asked.

'Non. I'm sorry.'

She shook her head, then smiled again and pushed the plate to me.

'On the house.'

I straightened up.

'Non. Non. Merci. I will bring you the money. I just live across the street.'

56

'Is OK,' she said, her voice soft. She went about her business as another customer stepped up and ordered a crêpe.

I stepped back and grabbed the plate, letting him pass. Soon a few other people were standing there, and I stepped further back to watch them, the crêpe cooling in my hands.

Then, I bit into it. And the world dropped away.

I don't know what Proust's voice sounded like, but in that moment, I could hear him in my head – speaking English with a thick French accent, telling me, emphatically, how eating madeleines affected him. They'd taken him immediately to his childhood. And somehow, eating crêpes with sugar and lemon was taking me into his childhood too! I was seeing little French toys and fussy dresses and flowers in tall vases. There was the creaking of old wooden floors, sunlight from high windows, crystal chandeliers!

When this vision subsided, I stood there stunned. Time had passed. Or I'd been in some kind of time worm hole. The other people had taken their crêpes away and I went back to the counter and asked for two more. The lady laughed and made them for me. I pigged out on French crêpes with sugar and lemon, and she took my twenty and gave me back fourteen euros. We now had a bond. I loved this woman.

Reluctantly, I had to move on. I pledged I'd be back for breakfast tomorrow and the day after that too. She laughed, covering her mouth in a sweet, shy way as if she were a girl of fourteen and waved.

~

The Pompidou was not hard to miss. The sheer scale of it made Paris look like some tiny town around it. You could see this building for miles. It must have been thirty, forty stories high and that's when I noticed that Paris did not, as a rule, have many skyscrapers. Looking this up on my phone I discovered there were strict rules governing the height of buildings. Tall buildings ruined the character of the place, apparently. Well, this place sure had it.

The first thing I wanted to do was ride the huge escalator on the outside. It was like a giant clear plastic gerbil tube if the gerbil was the size of six human beings. It went from the bottom outside corner and crossed diagonally to the top. It was thrilling. I went down three times. The views were spectacular. I gathered there were exhibitions inside this building, of art, and who knew what else. There could be movie theaters. Shopping malls. Golf courses. Skateparks. Perhaps an indoor beach? Such things happened in California. But I didn't much care what was going on inside. The building itself just bowled me over. When I got back to the bottom, I decided to walk around the whole thing. It was a long walk.

I was dying of thirst by the time I reached the other side of the building, where there was a very large piazza. And it looked like yet another town. A town of performers! Crowds of people had gathered around to see dancers, singers, artists drawing murals on the ground in chalk. There were face painters, artists selling their wares, craftsmen, weavers, people selling plants, skateboarders skateboarding, and there were people standing perfectly still, painted head to toe in silver or gold paint. Human statues. I got out my camera. Fingers itching.

But it was the faces of the audience that I took pictures of. Children trying to understand why the human statues didn't move. Teenagers teasing the human statues, trying to get them to move. Old people shaking their heads. Probably appalled at the waste of time and energy. Mostly, though, there was wonder in people's faces. In these times of instant entertainment and impressive technology, there was something timeless about one human being trying to make another submit to the wonder of astonishment with a simple trick, a costume, a skill. This art of performing in the street had been going on for perhaps thousands of years, and it was still in evidence here. It felt worthy of trying to capture on film. Could I catch that moment when a person's defenses came down and their face radiated the surprise?

I experimented with timing. Position. Distance. Lighting. Shadows. My approach had to be unobtrusive, or defenses would go up again. People hated cameras and photographers. For good reason. It was an intrusion of their privacy. They had every reason to be suspicious. *What was this stranger taking my picture for? What's in it for him?* I found it easier to find a spot where I could zoom in on a face from far away, where it wasn't obvious I was taking a person's picture. It took some practice, but I got better at it over time.

When I finally looked up, the sun was high in the sky. I was hot, sweaty, and tired, and I was still only on the outside of the Pompidou. I looked for some shade under one of the big plane trees and saw an amazing sight there. A group of performers sat together in a circle talking, taking a break. One of the human statues was there. A tall silver man. He was chewing gum. A man in a bear suit, his bear head sitting beside him on the ground was talking with him. He had a full beard and looked like a bear himself. A costume was hardly needed. I wondered how being a bear entertained people. He was laughing and smoking a pipe. Then there was – and I had to strain to see, I couldn't believe my eyes – someone who looked like Madonna. Yep. A skinny older Madonna with a pointy bra. When I stepped a bit closer, I could see it was a man. Next to him was a tall black woman wearing a man's suit from another century, her hair tucked under a bowler hat. She might have passed for a man except for the elegant features of her decidedly feminine face. High cheekbones. A slender neck. She turned to look at me, adjusting her round glasses and then leaned over to speak to an Asian man. When he saw me, he stood up and took a step toward me.

'Puis-je vous aider?' he said.

'Oh! I'm sorry to bother you. I was just looking for a little shade.'

'Pull up a chair,' came a voice from behind me. A short woman with straight hair cropped chin length then threw cans of pop to each one of the others. She was strong. And had a good aim. There was a rickety chair just outside their circle and I went over to it and dragged it closer.

'American?' asked the tall woman. She was smoking a cigar.

'Oui,' I said and smiled, eyeing the drinks.

From my seat, I could see two other members of this group. One was a man who appeared to be a mime artist. Hadn't seen a mime in a long time. Hadn't they gone out of fashion? The other was a woman of indeterminable age, dressed in old, faded clothing and wearing sturdy leather sandals. She was a pale-skinned with blonde dreadlocks. She saw me staring at her and waved. I waved back.

'What's your name?' she asked.

'I'm Grant Decker. Originally, from California. But I live in the UK now. In Cornwall.'

They all stopped eating and stared at me. Then they stared at the short woman.

'What are you doing here, Grant? In Paris?' she said, then sipped her drink.

'I'm a photographer. Looking for inspiration.'

'You want a drink?' the statue said, holding up a can.

'Oh, much obliged.' I stood up and took a step toward him. It was rather surreal, his metallic skin. But I was powerfully thirsty. I took the can, popped the top and had a long, satisfying drink. 'Say, can I get you all something to eat? Is there a place to buy some food around here?'

They all looked at each other. Stunned. Perhaps it wasn't customary, but I wanted to spend time with these people, and we all needed lunch. I had plenty of cash.

'Come with me, Grant. We can get a pizza to share,' the short woman said. 'Right this way. We'll be back in ten minutes.'

Everyone else seemed pleased with this choice. Off we went.

'What are you dressed as? I'm sorry my French is so bad. I couldn't tell what you were performing.'

She smiled, indulging me.

'We'll speak English for you then. We don't mind the practice. I'm Joan of Arc.'

'Ahhhh. I can see that now. What sort of act are you doing?'

She wrinkled her nose. In this moment she reminded me of Katie, who was also short in stature, with a pert nose. It drove her crazy to be taken for 'cute.' Katie was a serious person and so was this Joan character. Her face hardened. She had taken offense at my question.

'I'm not acting. I'm gathering an army.'

This confused me, but it didn't seem like she wasn't kidding around. I decided to have an open mind.

'OK. How about the others? What are their names?'

We continued walking as she took her time, apparently trying to decide if I was worthy of knowing more about the group.

'There's Madonna ... and Freud.'

'Freud?' I was careful not to smile. 'In the suit?'

'Oui. And Bear ... Bruce Lee. Marcel ... and ... JC.'

'JC. The woman in sandals?'

'Yes. Jesus Christ. But I think she's a little mixed up.' Joan spoke in whispers now. 'Our Savior was a man, no?'

Now I stopped.

'And dead too, no?' I said.

She frowned at me.

'She's very much alive.'

'Is she crazy?'

Joan thought about this, or maybe she was translating English in her head.

'I don't think so. Non.'

We walked on. There was more to all this than I could understand. It was intriguing. A woman who thought she was Joan of Arc. A Jesus Christ impersonator who was a woman. A Madonna lookalike who was a man. A man claiming to be Bruce Lee. A man in a bear costume. And a woman who didn't look remotely like Dr Sigmund Freud, but carrying on like she was. We got to the pizza tents and ordered. While we waited, I asked Joan a bit more about JC.

'What is Jesus doing here? At the Pompidou, I mean.'

Joan shrugged.

'Trying to earn a bit of money. To eat.'

'But what does she do? To earn the money?'

'Sometimes she recites from the bible. People give her few coins.'

'What about the statue?'

'He does well, just standing still.'

'What's his name?'

'Bill. But he prefers we call him statue.'

Strange little group.

'How do you raise your army?'

She tipped her head at me and crossed her arms.

'How do you think?'

I blinked.

'I have no idea.'

'Day after day. Week after week. I give my speeches, tell the people what the voices have told me, and I try to get them to drive the English out of France.'

I stared hard at her and really could not tell if she was pulling my leg or if she honestly believed she was Joan of Arc. This intrigued me. I wondered if they might allow me to take pictures of them, working. It would be fascinating to see their faces become their characters. Could I capture that? Or perhaps find the moment when they let those characters go? She must be quite a serious young actress, determined to stay in character with me, even through lunch.

I clapped.

She smiled at me. 'You also hate the English?'

Might as well play along. 'Well, we Americans were at war with them a while back. Maybe you haven't heard.'

Joan's lips drew up in a beautiful smile. 'I'm glad. I don't think I could eat with you if you were English.'

Two pizzas were ready, and I took the boxes carrying them back the way we came, walking next to the actress playing Joan of Arc.

'What about the rest of them. Do they stay in character too?'

She shook her head at me, like I was the one with a screw loose. 'I don't understand all your words, Grant Decker.'

'Oh, right. Sorry.' *Maybe we were both a bit language confused.* Yet, I was compelled to hang about and learn more about this little band of performers. It might be just the opportunity I was looking for. A puzzle to solve. Something to explore with my camera.

We got back to the little band of actors under the tree who welcomed the lunch. It seemed they were appreciative of my gesture. They each took a piece of a large pizza and there were grunts of joy.

I sat next to Dr. Freud. The tall woman in the suit.

'Joan says you speak English?'

'A bit.'

'What's your act? What do you do for money?'

She finished her bite of pizza and tutted. 'Americans. You are so obsessed with what others do for a living.' Then she took another bite.

Holy Cow. These actors were really something. Did they all stay in character like this? I wanted pictures of all of them.

'I like to do a photographic portrait of you. Of each one in your group?' I stood up and they all glanced over to me. 'I'm a photographer. Could I do portraits of you? All of you. Separately. As you work.'

'Will you pay us?' asked Bear, still chewing on his slice.

I swallowed. I did have some funds from the grant that I could use for this.

'Yes. Ten euros each. For today and tomorrow.'

They all looked at one another.

'Twelve,' Bear said.

'Done.'

I sat down and we all finished the meal as I imagined what I might be like, trying to photograph each of them as they worked. This was going to be fun.

~

The easy ones were the statue and the mime artist. These guys could hold a pose. But they wouldn't talk to me. They would not break character, I suppose. I had to respect that. I was very curious to learn about all these actors but getting someone to speak to me in English was going to be tricky.

Madonna, as it turned out, was the most fluent in my language and quite willing to tell me things. He explained he wasn't trans, just a man who liked being Madonna.

'I'm a queer man, honey.'

He said it was proper to call him *she/her*. She sang *Like a Virgin*, and afterwards, I applauded. Then she filled me in on this little family of actors and how they came to be. I took pictures as she talked.

'I'd been here about six months when I got to talking to Dr. Freud. He's actually pretty good at what he does.'

'I noticed he's a she.'

'Yeah. Same situation. She's a dyke named Donna, but that's all she'll say about the matter. She too likes to dress up and become someone else. In her case, Dr. Sigmund Freud.'

'Wow. Well. Do people here pay her, I mean him, for advice?'

'Yeah. They do. All he must do is put up this little sign. It says,' THE DOCTOR IS IN.' A chair. A little table. Bingo. Clients. People tell him the craziest stuff. And he gives good advice. He's got a degree in it. Psychology. I think he said that. Weird, eh?'

'Just seems a strange place to practice.'

'Does it?'

She gave me a wicked smile. A bit of mascara was running down her cheek from the hot sun. She took out a bottle of water from her bag and had a drink. Then offered some to me.

'No, thanks.' I took more pictures of her. She looked nothing like Madonna, of course. But the wig, the false eyelashes, the pointy bra, all created the illusion and somehow you believed it, especially when she danced and sang. She was good at it.

'How much do you make in a day?'

'You Americans! So rude! I'd never ask you that!'

'Sorry. Sorry.' I took another picture. She was photogenic. That was good.

'We make enough, for the lot of us, anyway.'

'How long have you been together then?'

She laughed.

'You make it sound like we're married. It's not like that. People come and go. I've been here a year, maybe more. We've all found places to live near here. We're friends *and* co-workers.' She straightened up and looked into the sky. 'Liberty, Equality, Fraternity! Vive La France!'

'Wow. That's great. But what are you hoping for?'

She let out an exasperating breath.

'You mean me? Or everyone?'

'Start with you.'

'An acting job. Or singing job, of course. We all want the same thing. Well. Let's see. Bruce and I do, anyway. We are lookalikes. Bruce can do a bit of martial arts. I can sing.'

'What about the bear guy?'

'Oh. He's ... special. He just wants to be an animal.'

'OK. And people pay him for that?'

'Day and *night*, my love. Day and *night*. But don't you dare ask him about his night job. You don't really want to know.'

I lowered my camera.

'I don't?'

'It's kinda violent. His business. Not yours. Got it?'

'Right.'

'What about the mime guy? What's his name?'

'Marcel?'

'You're kidding.'

'No, that's really his name. Marcel. But we don't discuss last names. Ever. Better that way.'

'Does he get paid here?'

'Honey, this is about the only place in the *world* where Marcel can earn a few euros a day being a mime artist.'

'I would imagine so. I thought all the mimes died or something.'

'Marcel thinks so too. He's convinced it was a virus. And only *he* escaped.'

'Oh? Why is that?'

I snapped more pictures. All this information was helping me try to understand these individuals. People were naturally protective of their true natures. The ultimate challenge of portrait photography was to put people at ease. As Madonna talked and offered her theories about her friends, I could tell she *wanted* me to know her and her perspectives on her friends. Her face was incredibly expressive of emotion. There was empathy as she talked. A wise understanding. It shined through the make-up.

'He doesn't know,' she said. 'It bothers him, but he's just trying to live with it, you know? Like a condition he has, that he can't help. He doesn't have answers for it. None of us do.'

'So, he talks to you?'

She threw back her head and I could see her Adam's apple bobbing up and down as she laughed. She covered her big teeth with bony hands. 'Marcel never, ever, talks, Chéri. He *mimes*. He can mime anything.'

'Gee. Maybe *he* has a virus.'

She laughed again and punched my arm. It hurt.

'Could be. But nobody has caught it from him. Poor thing. He has the hardest time. No doubt about it. We all chip in a little for his food.'

'What about the woman in sandals. She really thinks she's Jesus?'

'Oh, yeah. I worry about her the most.'

'More than Joan?'

Madonna blinked at me.

'Joan super believes in her voices. But she's angry at the world for being cowardly. Jesus just *loves* everybody. In a *platonic* way, of course. Not very entertaining, to tell the truth. She'd starve if we didn't throw a little food her way.'

'Does she need help? I mean mentally?'

'Don't we all? We're just doing our best here, Grant. We help each other out a bit. We're artists. Performers. Perfecting our craft in the great tradition of all artists who come to Paris to BE artists.'

'Right. I get it. Like Hemingway.'

I took a few more pictures until Madonna got up again and stood on her platform, turned on her boom box and brought the microphone up to her lips. She sang the opening bars of *Material Girl*. People stopped and listened. Laughed. Then they clapped and sang along with this skinny man in a skirt and heels, shaking his booty in a golden bra and a wig. Madonna was electrified by the crowd's interest. She shimmied and danced around. How she managed the chunky heels amazed me, but this man was happy in his own skin, in *his* material world. When I gazed at the pictures on my digital camera, I saw there were some good ones. You couldn't always tell if Madonna was a man or a woman. It didn't matter. You saw Madonna coming through another person's face and *that* was interesting.

Chapter Five

That night I had a phone call from Leslie. It was good to hear her voice. It still felt a bit strange to be in her flat, living in her Paris life.

'Are you finding the glamour, Grant? Isn't it amazing?'

'Oui! I rode the metro everywhere yesterday, to get a feel for the vastness of Paris.'

'The metro! Well, how'd that work out for you?'

'Good. I'm going back there to take pictures. But I've also found some interesting people I'm doing portraits of at the Pompidou!'

'Oh. Well. Amazing. Long as you're getting inspired. How's Madame Garnier?'

'Oh, she's fine...'

'Katie told me about the robbery. What a shame.'

'Yes. Madame Garnier let me in and gave me her keys so I could get them copied. She's quite a character, isn't she?'

'She is, indeed. Well, don't get put off by the bad start. Get out and see things, Grant. There's so much history there! Go see the islands!'

'I'm doing that today.'

'Good. And take walks. Lots of walking. Hemingway did that. He walked all over the city!'

'I notice you have quite a few books about him.'

'Oh, I love his writing. Not the man, mind you, but the writing. That was really something.'

'Thanks for all this, Leslie. It's an amazing opportunity.'

'A world away from Cornwall, isn't it?'

'It sure is. Though, I'd say there are some similarities too. Some free spirits here, like there.'

'Oh, that's a good angle! I'm dying to see the pictures.'

74

'I will show you when I get back,' I said. 'When I've had a chance to edit them and think about what I'm trying to do here. It'll take time. I'm doing my best.'

'I know you are, Grant. I have faith in you.'

That somehow sounded a little ominous.

'Well, I better get out there while the light is good.'

'Yes! Au revoir, mon Chéri!'

'Au revoir!'

After pushing the hang-up button on my phone, I felt my muscles tightened up. What exactly would my boss be expecting to see? I thought of all those scruffy children and old men carrying wine bottles in the streets from the 1950s. No. Imitating great photographers was not the way. I had to follow my own instincts about what to photograph. I would explore this new world with my own eyes. There was no telling what other people would make of my pictures, but I had to risk being original, to please myself in the hopes that it would lead to art.

~

The next morning, I was standing before the crêpe lady, staring above her head at the list of crêpes. I could not decide. I wanted the citron again. She could tell I did. Yet, here in Paris, it seemed vital to try something new every day.

'Strawberries and crème,' she said. She had decided for me. She winked.

'Oui, Madame.' She hadn't steered me wrong yet.

The crêpe lady got busy, and I watched, mesmerized at how she did it, like a dance. Full of energy. Precise. Not at all mechanical. She was in tune with her magic.

When I bit into the flat pancake of flour, egg, and butter, with the strawberries bursting in my mouth, the sugar and whipped cream bringing in their flavors too, a hint of vanilla, I felt like I had been shot out of a cannon and had crashed on the moon. It was like that 1902 short film by George Méliès. It made my *heart* beat faster, that film. It was a dream, perhaps THE dream of lunar exploration before we worked out how to get there. It was dreamy. Like this crêpe with strawberries and crème.

'Merci, merci, merci, Madame. My name is Grant. What is your name?'

'Marie.'

'Merci, Marie. Your crêpes are a dream.'

'Merci, Grant.'

She glowed. I was feeling a fondness for Marie. It wasn't just great crêpes, though that of course, helped. It was the way she did it and that beautiful smile afterwards. It all worked together to enchant me. After I finished my meal there was no excuse to hang about. She had other customers. So, I waved to Marie and headed toward the Seine.

Today, I was going to those islands. I wanted to see them. I'd spent hours last night reading books on Hemingway. He walked around Paris a lot, at night, and he walked on these little islands. It was the center of Medieval Paris! Where it all began! I wanted to walk it too, and I was going to find the place on one of the islands where Héloïse and Abélard's love story began. These famous Paris lovers were a very big deal here. People still went to visit their grave. What romantics!

It was another glorious day in Paris. Warm and wonderful. Or do you just feel that way after eating one of Marie's crêpes? Who knows? I was going to enjoy it anyway. My camera around my neck, my keys in my pocket, I was on day three and getting the hang of things. I wasn't scared anymore. And as I walked, I noticed that NOBODY had a pack on their back! All the tourists, and there were a lot of them heading for these islands, were prepared.

Walking across one of the five bridges, the noise of cars fell away and it grew quiet. The scale of this little island was small. It felt *intimate*. The narrow streets ran through the dumpling shape of it. There was a street with a lane of traffic on each side of the island and one running through the middle. Four narrow roads ran across. There were beautiful old residences, some restored, others left run down, but even they were elegant as old ruins could be. Down the center were little shops displaying food or art objects inside that took your breath away. And there was gelato, on every corner, it seemed, and the competition was fierce for getting the richest, most exotic flavors possible. Long lines of people were waiting for their turn and looking happy even in their anticipation.

It was July. The height of the tourist season. I was on the smaller of the two islands, Île Saint-Louis. The bigger island, Île de la Cité, had Notre Dame on it, but this one had a church too and hearing the bells here, so clearly, so close, made the air vibrate. The stillness after they stopped was a profound contrast and it made me think about the nature of time. Bells marked time, like photography did. And here I was in time, standing on the place where Paris once began.

Surveying the island with my feet didn't take long, but I enjoyed ambling down the little streets and picturing the way life might have been five or six hundred years ago, the way the shops might have looked, and people selling wine and cheese, as they did now. I crossed over one of the small bridges and was impressed by the scale and inventiveness of Notre Dame, picturing Victor Hugo as he cast his eyes over it, imaging the character of a hunchback. The gargoyles were impressive too and I could see their attraction as photography models, the embodiment of the shadow of fear and superstition that hung over the city, dominating the population, and keeping them in check.

Later, after a coffee, I checked my map and found the place on the island where there was another kind of landmark, the house where Héloïse and Abélard found true love in the twelfth century. I kept finding more about them on my phone and became entranced by their story. They'd been called the Romeo and Juliet of France. Star-crossed lovers. Abélard was not only a monk and teacher, but also a famous philosopher in his day. He learned about a young lady of noble birth, Héloïse, who knew Latin, Greek and Hebrew and had a deep thirst for knowledge. He convinced her uncle, who was her guardian and lived on the Île de la Cité, to let him tutor her. One thing led to another and when the uncle found out the tutor had taught his niece about the delights of love, he separated them with heavy threats. But they continued to meet in secret. She became pregnant by Abélard, and he took her to Brittany to have their child. Abélard suggested a secret marriage to appease the uncle and keep his prospects positive in the church, which Héloïse reluctantly agreed to. The secret was not kept by her uncle, however, and she chose to publicly deny it. Her life was made so difficult she had to go to a nunnery. The uncle, feeling the family must be avenged, sent his sons to castrate Abélard. He survived the ordeal, but from then on, he and

Héloïse lived separate lives, he in a monastery and she in a nunnery.

The letters of Héloïse and Abélard did not surface until over a hundred years after their death. They were saved by Héloïse and passed on after her death, later copied and this love story lived on thanks to the copies made and passed on as a historical record. They remain an important thread in the tapestry of French identity. Scholars and writers have been fascinated by the letters which showed quite a different story than the one of a young girl seduced by her teacher. These two were intellectual equals, both seduced by the power of love. While initially drawn together to explore the full range of that love, they ended up living their lives separately in institutions that valued the mind over the carnal desires of the body. They were, however, buried together in the Père Lachaise cemetery in Paris, their final resting place and a place that still inspires lovers.

I thought about this as I wandered around and found a gelato place to contemplate love.

Two scoops. Coffee and vanilla. Héloïse and Abélard. I pulled out my phone again to call Katie.

'Hello?'

'Hi, sweetheart! It's me! Your Abélard!'

'My what?'

'I'm here! On the Île de la Cité, eating gelato, like the Parisians of old.'

She laughed.

'I don't think they had gelato in the time of Héloïse and Abélard, but I read somewhere that in the sixth century a Roman governor was living there.'

'Gladiator Gelato then!'

'Probably.'

'How are you and Ariel?'

'Oh, we're doing all right. The weather's nice here.'

'Really? Or are you just saying that because you're jealous?'

'Both.'

I loved my wife's laugh. I'd do just about anything to hear it.

'I'm coming back here and bringing you with me. It is *soooo* romantic here.'

'I'd like that. Have you been taking pictures?'

'Yes. LOTS of them. And I've met some crazy interesting people.'

'In Paris? Who'd have thought!'

'I met some young actors. Very unusual.'

'Oh? And you're photographing them?'

'Uh huh, and get this. They *never* break character. There's a statue guy, Joan of Arc, Dr. Sigmund Freud, who is a woman, a mime, a bear, Bruce Lee, and Madonna—'

'Jesus.'

'Oh, yes! And Jesus. I almost forgot her.'

'Her?'

'It's complicated.'

'You aren't getting into any trouble, are you?'

'Moi?'

She chuckled now.

'You are learning French, I see.'

'Oui. It is a-mazing how much French there is in English.'

'Right. Well, I'm glad you got things sorted and are having fun now.'

'Oh, yes. Money, passport, wallet, keys. It's all great now. I rode the metro lines. All of them. I know what's what.'

'That's marvelous, dear. I'm proud of you. And you're finding people to photograph too. Leslie will be thrilled.'

'I've talked with her.'

'Good. She has high hopes for you.'

'I'm doing my best. I miss you. I just wanted to tell you how nice it was on this little island and how I'm imagining you by my side, having a lick of my gelato and wishing like mad that you were here.'

'Mon cher mari,' she said. 'That's ... my dear husband.'

'Ma petite Chérie.' I was working from a cheat sheet I'd made for this call.

'Oooh la, Mon amour.'

'Ma petite ... crêpe du citron.'

She kissed the phone.

'That's sweet, Ma bête sexy.'

'Mon adorable animal ballon.'

'I'm your little balloon animal?'

'You know how I love balloon animals.'

'True. Well, my big-eyed goldfish, I better get back to work.'

'Right. Me too. Take care, my love. And kiss the princess for me.'

'I will. We'll call you tomorrow night. She wants to talk with you.'

'Oui!' I kissed the phone with gelato lips as the person near me turned around and frowned at me like I was some uncouth peasant. This became my cue to leave.

As I traipsed across a different bridge, I remembered the French word for a carefree wanderer. A *flaneur!* This was what I would do now. Wander. I soon found myself before a strange and beautiful window. It was a store that sold paper. There were several huge picture windows each featuring a gorgeous display of thick, luxurious sheets. What it was used for, I didn't have a clue, but was astounded to learn I could get excited about paper.

In one display, there was a fish print. A huge dead fish must have been painted with deep blue paint and then carefully laid on the paper, pressed and then removed to reveal an imprint of fish, the scales and weight of it, revealed by the glorious paper. It was exquisite. In another window, there were stacks of smaller sizes of paper and then beautiful little bottles of ink, all in a row. Then pens were lined up like little soldiers. Did people write letters like this still? I noticed wax sticks and matches and marvelous seals. It made me want to write with these things. Thank goodness the shop was closed, but I took pictures. I'd never seen such a beautiful display that made we want to touch. Texture. This is what I wanted to work on next with my pictures.

I walked on and heard more church bells. This too was not something I had ever experienced in LA, but I liked hearing them. Churches were everywhere. I stopped in my tracks when I saw a man in priestly Catholic robes down to his ankles, walking ahead of me, as if it was the most normal thing in the world. This was not normal in *my* world, but I could imagine there had been men of the cloth walking down these same streets for centuries.

After lunch, I hurried to the place where I was supposed to meet a man who was going to take me to the catacombs. I was going UNDER Paris now. I'd been emailing him for weeks, a friend of Leslie's, he said he could take me there on a tour. His name was Pierre. When I saw him standing by the locked gate, I worried that we weren't going to get in today. Sometimes they let you in and sometimes they didn't, he'd said. He only took one or two people at a time. I had my camera ready.

Pierre stood up to his full height of six feet and smiled broadly. Then he shook my hand. We greeted one another and he assured me the tour was on. The guard unlocked the gate for us, and we went down a rickety metal staircase that spiraled and spiraled around until I thought I was going to be sick. It was a long way down. One hundred and thirty-one steps, my guide informed me. About two hundred feet below sea level. It got progressively more humid and smelled like wet dirt. I was already wishing the hour-long tour was over.

It was dark too, with just the occasional light bulb above our heads to light the way. We could only walk single file and Pierre had the flashlight, which he pointed to the ghastly views both left and right, for on each side of us were continuous rows of stacked bones: femurs, skulls, or both, stacked from floor to ceiling. In the 18th century there'd been major public health problems tied to the city cemeteries, and the long-term plan was to remove the bones to these underground caves. It was like walking in a huge burial pit, only the bones were strangely, lovingly, respectfully, and artfully arranged. The patterns were so odd. Decorative. Like rug patterns. Yet no amount of festive decoration could alter the fact that you were looking at the remains of real people. Centuries of them! They'd been born and had died and were now being stored down here and on display, for a small fee. The sight of those bones will haunt me forever. I took pictures. How could I not? But I knew they were not the pictures I wanted to see. Photographers always take pictures of grim things. Is it out of curiosity? Or is there some kind of beauty there that is revealed? I could think of a few photographers who pushed boundaries with their depiction of ugly beauty. Joel-Peter Witkin came to mind. As I trudged along the endless path of death, I asked myself. What are photographs for?

Certainly, one purpose was to capture curiosities. The unusual. Things you don't see every day. Or to create them. We look because we can't turn away from both the deeply ugly and the beautiful. Diane Arbus understood this, and I admire her work. Her daughter too. Amy Arbus. We also look to understand. To see details and make sense of things. And we take photographs to see what is *rarely* seen. We want to know, and we want to distract ourselves from really knowing.

If this underground cave was the scene of a battle, I would be horrified at the scale of the loss of life, but death didn't happen to these people in an instant or in a month or a year. This place was a living record of the life and death of hundreds of thousands of people over many years. As I was thinking about this, a drop of water fell on my head, and I looked up to the inky blackness of the earth above me. For a moment I was rigid with fear. It was like being buried alive and I called out to Pierre.

'How much longer!'

'It's all right. Very normal to get disoriented down here. We've only been walking a few minutes. Another fifty minutes to go.'

I could hardly believe it. The bones went on and on. I couldn't make sense of anything Pierre was saying now. His words just turned to mush in my head. All I could do was count my steps. There was no going back, only forward. I had to calm myself like a frightened child. Think of something happy, I told myself. Think of getting out of here.

After what seemed like hours, we came at long last to the staircase that would get us out. I was shaking with relief. The scene had not changed the whole hour. There was not a sliver of space, no relief, no variety to the scene. It was bones and more bones of the dead along the entire path, and I could not guess how deep the caves were reaching out from the path on either side. The bones just went back to what looked like infinity. It was sobering. Here they all were, these dead people, kept in the largest file drawer of bones on the planet! I knew there would be bones in these catacombs, but I'd never imagined the scale of it.

Pierre told me they'd kept the bones in old, unused, underground quarries at first. Then whole sections of Paris collapsed, and it had to be reconfigured. That's when they made bone storage vaults and started the stacking. When Haussman was doing his major rearrangement of Paris to get rid of all the slums, he organized it underground for more bones. Amazingly, there are still quite a few cemeteries left in Paris that survived the bone collecting. Some beautiful ones, I'm told.

When we got to the top, to sunlight and fresh air, I gasped in relief and hugged Pierre like the American I was. He laughed and patted my back awkwardly.

'You all right, Grant?'

'That was morbid, Pierre. Thank you.'

He laughed again.

'Did you get some pictures?'

'I think so. The light was low, but I'll look at them later and try to see what I got.'

'What do you feel like doing now?'

In truth I wanted to climb into bed with Katie and hold her tight. Life! My life! My wife and daughter! I just wanted to be home with them again. But I composed myself. Instead, I yelled out the next thing that came to mind.

'I want to buy shoes!' My arms were outstretched. 'Point me in the right direction!'

He took me out into the sunshine.

'Over there. I'll leave you to your shopping then,' he said.

'Thank you, Pierre.'

He ambled off and I found a café.

I wanted a coffee, by myself, to take my pulse and write in my sketchbook.

Sitting down, I found my pulse was indeed a little fast. This had been an adventure all right but depressing too. It was the kind of thing that made you want to live fully each day and seek out the company of living people. After my coffee, I headed over to the Pompidou to see how my new friends were doing.

Chapter Six

It was around six in the evening when I got to the Pompidou and the crowds were thinning out. Statue man was stretching under a tree. He'd clearly put in a long day and was tired. Bear was flat on his back on the ground, his bear suit beside him. His face shiny from sweat. How he managed it in this heat, I couldn't imagine. Madonna was drinking wine and Dr. Freud was folding up her table.

'Look who's back!' shouted Joan of Arc. She ran over to me and jumped into my arms, winding her short limbs around my body. She weighed almost nothing, so it wasn't hard on me, but it took me by surprise.

'Hello to you too!'

'Are you bored of Paris already?' asked Bruce Lee, who walked by me and smiled.

'Oh, no. Not at all. I saw the catacombs today.'

'The catacombs!' This got Bear to sit up. 'How cheerful! Must have been hot down here,' he said.

JC appeared, as if from a tomb herself.

'Did I miss something?'

'Grant went to see the bones,' Bruce said.

'Where?' she asked.

'The catacombs. You know.'

'Oh ... right. How ghastly!' She wrinkled her nose.

'It *was* terrible.' I admitted. 'Interesting, but terrible. I needed a bit of cheering up, so I thought I'd come by and take you all out for a bite to eat and a drink.' The truth was I didn't understand French food at all and needed people to help me decide what to eat. I had a generous food budget that went a long way with this group. Like me, they didn't have epicurean tastes.

'Let's go. I'm ready!' Bear said and got to his feet. 'Coming, Marcel? Statue?'

The mime artist and the statue nodded emphatically and got their things.

'Yes!' cried Dr. Freud. 'The doctor is OUT!'

Everyone fell in and we started walking.

'Where we going?' I asked.

Everyone stopped and looked to Bear.

'If we go to the Hide, I'll have to wear my suit. I don't want my boss to see me, or he'll start yelling.'

'Not if we get a table down below,' Madonna said. 'Come on, Bear. We want to show Grant where you work!'

He moaned, just like a bear.

'It's nothing glamorous!' he said to me.

'I'd like to see it,' I countered, and everyone cheered.

'We like to go there, but Bear is embarrassed by us.'

'No ... I'm just afraid you'll all get too drunk and get me fired.'

'Come on! We'll be on our best behavior, and we promise to leave early, right?' JC tried to catch everyone's eye. The peacemaker. 'We must get our sleep anyway. Tomorrow is our busy day.'

'Let's go, already!' shouted Bear.

JC rolled her eyes, locked arms with the Doctor and Joan and off we went. Joan was in good spirits I noticed.

'Did you get any recruits today?' I asked as she practically bounced along beside me on the pavement.

'Oui. A whole group of students agreed to fight with me. A group of radicals!'

'Oh? Did they put a bit of money in your bucket?'

'They did. They were Spanish. They want to evict the English from their country too. It seems too many of the English have bought holiday homes there.'

'Oh, dear. I've heard that too.'

'No one much likes the English,' Joan said and smiled. 'How about you, Dr. Freud?'

'Me? Well. I like many of them. Like you, for instance.' She smiled widely and pushed her spectacles up her nose. 'The English gave me a home when Germany got too dangerous for me and my family.'

'I have nothing against the English if they stay in their own country!' cried Joan. She turned to me. 'They can visit France, of course. But they can't have it!'

'Quite right.'

~

We got to club HIDE, which had a glowing neon sign. Hardly a place that went unnoticed, but even the color didn't do much to make it an attractive establishment. It looked, like everything around it, as if it had been there since the last mid-century. We went into a dark cavern of a place and for a moment I thought I was back underground.

Bear pushed me along and I let Joan take my hand and lead me down some stairs to a corner lit by candles, a snug big enough for all of us. We moved around the edges of a large square wooden table and sat down. The candlelight made everyone look dreamlike, even Statue, with his sharp angular features. He was a different man without metallic paint on his face.

'Why do you go by Statue?' I asked. 'It makes you seem like a stranger.'

He raised his shoulders and lowered them again.

'I believe *you* are the stranger here.'

Then he picked up a menu and covered his face.

'Ignore him, Grant,' Joan said. 'He is rude when he opens his mouth.'

'Did you guys see that huge dog today?' asked Madonna.

'It barked at me!' Joan said.

'Standard poodle. Gorgeous,' said Bear. 'I like them.'

'You would,' Joan said. 'It was your size!'

'There was a water balloon fight today too. Anyone see that? It was so hot,' Bruce said. 'It's going to be hotter tomorrow.'

'Where are you going tomorrow, Grant?' asked Madonna. 'You should go somewhere cool and fun.'

'Well, just about anywhere is going to be more fun than the catacombs,' Bear said.

'It's true. It *was* depressing. I suppose you guys have been there.'

All of them laughed.

'Tourist stuff. We don't do that. It costs money,' Bruce said.

The waiter came and took everyone's orders. Then went away.

'You know what? I'm going take a day off tomorrow and take Grant to some places. It's too hot for me to dance around all day tomorrow anyway,' Madonna said.

'But you'll miss out on the money,' JC said and looked worried.

It was quiet all around the table for a moment.

'I could pay you something to be my tour guide for the day. Would ten euros be all right?'

Statue threw down the menu and stormed off.

'Don't worry about him,' Madonna said. 'He is easily offended.'

'Oh! I'm sorry. Did I offend you with that offer?'

'It was really very sweet of you to offer me money to show you around. But non. It would be my pleasure. I can handle a day off work. It's fine.'

'Well, thank you,' I said. 'It's kind of you

And it was all settled. Not long after, the drinks came, and everyone guzzled theirs. We sat in pleasant silence for a few minutes.

'Hey, Grant?' Bear put his face close to mine. 'We're all taking Bastille Day off. How about we meet you at noon at the old menagerie? It's a favorite place of ours. You'll like it. A very old place. With lovely animals.'

Everyone clapped, excited like little children.

'It's lovely,' Dr. Freud said. 'A small-scale zoo.'

'Wonderful!'

We shared some chili, chips, soup, and bread along with the beers and wine and talked into the night about revolutions, kings, queens, and rock and roll. Dr. Freud launched into a rather eloquent musing about La Belle Époque. I marveled at how even under the influence of spirits, Donna, the woman playing Freud, was completely in character, thoroughly believable as the man who had visited Paris during the 1889 Exposition World Fair.

'We still need to see off the English,' grumbled Joan into her beer, also completely in character.

Chapter Seven

The next day, bright and early, I picked up Madonna at the Pompidou, and we went out for breakfast to her favorite bakery, Boulangerie Utopie. I didn't expect her to wear Madonna clothing if she wasn't performing on the piazza, but clearly, even on her day off, she identified as Madonna. She wore the usual make-up—the heavy fake eyelashes, clumpy mascara, ruby red lipstick. Taking out a compact, she powdered her nose as soon as we sat down. Eyes in the cafe followed her every move, as if she might be the real one. Having coffee. Here.

'May I take pictures of you today, on your day off?' I asked, while we waited for our buns and coffee.

'Of course, mon Chéri!' She batted her eyelashes at me, and twisted her fingers through her hair, visibly excited by my attention. It made me a bit uncomfortable. What exactly had I got myself into? I put both my big hands on the marble table and stared at them.

'I feel compelled to tell you, Madonna, that I am a happily married man.'

She threw her head back with a deep throaty chuckle. Apparently, she found this entertaining.

'Oh, go on. You're safe with me, honey. I've got a boyfriend.'

She crossed her skinny legs and let out a huff, tucking a piece of her blonde wig into a headscarf. I dropped my shoulders and relaxed. Today Madonna was wearing sandals with a thin silk dress that was clinging to her emaciated body. She wore a loose knit jumper over it. and was draped in costume jewelry—paste diamonds and a beaded necklace.

I stood up and took a few pictures of her as our food arrived. The place looked like it hadn't changed since the nineteen forties. The furniture was diner era. Retro. The coffee was served in thick, restaurant style white mugs, the kind I recalled from America with two thin green lines at the top and one at the bottom. It surprised me, seeing these objects from what I considered to be *my* American past, here in Paris.

The pastries were eye popping. Not at all from the past but quite modern. I'd never seen anything like them. Madonna had chosen a black swirly bun with seeds and icing sugar. She pulled off a piece for me to try. It tasted of cardamom and carraway seeds. I opted for a long, frosted bun that had, oddly, a grey custard inside. I had no idea what to make of it. I let Madonna try some and she gave it a shivering smile of approval. I ventured forth and found it delicious too. The coffee was also quite good. In a class by itself. I understood why she loved the place.

'Can you tell me a little more about JC?' I asked. 'Do you know her story?'

Madonna glanced at me over her coffee cup. She set it down and took a deep breath.

'I know everyone's story, ma Chéri59. We all have one.'

'I can't imagine she makes much money reciting the beatitudes on the piazza at Pompidou.'

'Non. Not a popular form of entertainment.'

'So why does she do it?'

Madonna raised her eyes to the ceiling and sighed.

'What a question. Have you talked to Dr. Freud?'

I sipped my own coffee and paused.

'About JC? No.'

'Hmmm. Well. She's not really Jesus Christ.' She sighed. 'I mean, goodness, what DO I mean?' She laughed. 'This is so confusing.'

'Go on. I'll try to follow.'

'Well, why would she pretend to be Jesus Christ, a man, when she is clearly a woman? Dr. Freud has talked to her about this. And it's a case of sibling rivalry. She believes she is the sister of Jesus Christ, Mary, who is pretending to be her brother Jesus, because she is jealous of his fame.'

'Wait. Jesus had a sister?'

'You don't hear much about it, but yes, Jesus had siblings. Can you imagine what that must have been like? I mean the second child of any family gets sidelined, but what if your older brother was claiming to be the son of God?'

I rubbed my forehead. This was getting convoluted. 'There's the whole problem of it being over 2000 years ago. Her relationship to Jesus is not the biggest problem she has.'

Madonna leaned closer.

'Exactly. We don't dwell on that.'

'Does Dr. Freud talk to her regularly?'

'She tries to. I mean ... he tries to. He says it is important not to upset her with accusations.'

'No, I imagine that would chase her away.'

'They've had some good talks. I think she's getting closer to accepting herself as someone of value, even if she isn't Jesus.'

'Really. Hmmm. And how close is Dr. Freud to accepting herself as someone of value even if she isn't Dr. Freud?'

Madonna blinked at me with her long eyelashes and pulled her shoulders back. I had crossed a line. I guess the thing that bonded all of them together was a loose grip on identity and trusting each other for acceptance no matter who they thought they were. She drank more coffee and wouldn't look at me.

'I'm sorry. I'm just trying to understand.'

She patted my hand and stared out the window.

'Don't worry about it. We each find our own way to be here in the now, Grant. And it doesn't require your understanding or approval.'

~

After we finished breakfast, we left the building and as we walked down the pavement, Madonna announced the plan. We were going to visit cemeteries.

I stopped.

'What? Please. No. Not more death.'

'Oh, non, non, non. Not death. Life! A world of difference from where you went underground. Trust me.

101

You'll enjoy it. I promise. Good pictures are to be had. We Parisians love our cemeteries.'

I was just glad she was speaking to me again and in a good mood. We hopped on the metro to go to Cimetière du Père Lachaise. It was further out from the inner arrondissements. Almost to the twentieth. I noticed that on the metro trains, ladies carried their tiny dogs in beautiful leather purses, like an accessory. And the dogs seemed quite happy to be there, looking marvelous, well combed and accepting treats from people. The French clearly loved their dogs and took them everywhere.

There was also the opportunity to observe the commuters again on these trains. Such serious faces. I experimented with taking pictures in the reflection of windows. The camera aimed away so that it wasn't obvious I was recording them. They didn't see me taking their picture. When people are deep in the privacy of their own thoughts, there is much to see in their faces. The boredom you assume is there, is not really boredom at all, but a ponderous review of their own thoughts, a frank and sober comparison of who they are compared with who they thought they'd become someday. Nobody looked happy about it. A carriage full of critical assessment.

Once we got off the train and entered the cemetery, the sounds from the street faded behind us. The trees were in full leaf and swaying slightly in the soft breeze of a summer day. Movement in the distance caught my eye, something coming toward us quite fast. It was a boy on a bicycle, approaching one of the paths crossing the cemetery. He arrived in front of us with the screech of his brakes.

'Regarde où tu vas, dèmon!' cried Madonna, throwing her hands in the air.

He glowered at her, breathless and angry, then cast a wary glance toward me. I must have looked like an American tourist because he started barking at me in English.

'Buy a map! One euro!' he cried, then pulled a neatly folded map out of his back pocket. 'Oscar Wild! Jim Morrison! Edith Piaf!'

Madonna folded her arms and looked heavenward.

'What do you think? Should I buy it?' I asked her.

'Buy it if you like. I don't care. A souvenir for your wife.'

Another French word. At least it sounded French to me. Souvenir.

'Can I take your picture?' I asked the boy, on impulse. Something about his face interested me.

'Two euros for my picture.'

Madonna rolled her eyes at his cheek.

'Pirate!' she yelled in his direction.

'Chef d'entreprise!' he yelled back.

'What's your name then?' I asked in a calm manner.

'Indigo,' he answered, matching my tone exactly. 'Take the picture.' He lifted his chin and struck a pose – a skinny boy beside his bike. Dark hair came down his forehead like a paint stroke, covering one eye, fine and straight. His hair was cut short in the back. His eyes were indigo blue like his name and shining with possibility. The energy behind them! The bike was an old 1990's model. A Schwinn Stingray. Another strange image from my American youth, surprising me by being here, in Paris. It was rusted and beat up. How did he go so fast on it?

'The light isn't good here. Come this way,' I said. 'Toward the sun.'

He followed me to a spot beside a large tombstone and let me position him with his bike, so the light revealed more details. I saw then that he was a boy of only seven or eight, yet his face was hardened by more experience than that. His shoulders were wide and his back straight. He watched me, with my camera, and stood as if he were braced for a storm. He was defiant. I snapped the picture.

'Thank you, Indigo.' I fished in my pocket for the three euros and placed them in his waiting hand. He stuffed the money in his pocket and retrieved the map for me, which I noticed now was worn at the edges. He'd been carrying it around in his sweaty pocket for some time. He mounted his bike and was off like a shot.

After unfolding it, I found I couldn't find much of anything. The words were all rubbed out.

'Do you know where Oscar Wilde is buried?' I asked Madonna.

'But of course! Follow me, mon Chéri.'

As we walked, it struck me how densely populated the cemetery was and how many of the tombs were above ground in little marble buildings. It was like a mini city of dead souls with some areas covered completely by long black shadows. It was a mirror of Paris, a metaphor, of the high-rise penthouses of the rich towering over the poor.

Many of the tombs had sculpture on them. Elaborate angels with detailed wings and robes, anguish on their faces. There were gargoyles too, guarding their charges. But Oscar Wilde's gravestone was modern. A simple slab of marble at ground level, with a highly stylized Art Nouveau angel above it. The wings were as long as the slab. And across the stone was the unmistakable imprint of kisses.

'People kiss his grave?'

'Oh, oui! All the time!'

As if to demonstrate, Madonna went over and wiped a spot with her handkerchief and planted her red lips. When she turned back to me, her eyes were wet.

'We ... *love* Oscar. He wanted to be buried here, with *us*.'

She thumped her chest.

Clearly, this was true. We stood there a long time, as other people came and touched the grave, heads bowed. Some kissed it. That his memory was still so alive and well, stunned me. Oscar Fingal O'Flahertie Wills Wilde was a complicated soul from Ireland whose struggles touched people all over the world. I took pictures of his grave. He'd touched me too.

'Jim Morrison is here?' I asked. She nodded. We walked slowly over to that grave too and found a young fan, dressed, appropriately enough, in the style of the sixties. She was squatting on her boot heels and weeping into her handkerchief. Fresh tears for another long dead poet. While his marker was not as elaborate as Wilde's, it still had fresh flowers and a weeping fan. I was impressed.

After that Madonna showed me the graves of Géricault and Delacroix and I admit I was star struck. That their bones rested in this quiet, beautiful place touched me. Each narrow avenue of tombs was like a row of little temples, and I suddenly understood the problem of running out of room. All the bones of all the people who had lived in Paris over centuries of time came to an awful lot of bones. London had the same problem. Not enough room for the dead. There were a great many plague pits and bones moved around as buildings continued rise in the city scape. The cemeteries had to give way, but the ones that remained each had their own unique beauty and atmosphere.

'Hey!' I stopped on the path and stared at Madonna. 'Aren't Héloïse and Abélard buried here somewhere?'

'Oui. In the far corner. You want to see them?'

'Oui! Merci!'

She laughed and took my hand, and we started walking. 'Such a romantic.'

It was a little cathedral-like house! Perhaps twelve feet by twelve feet. I slowed down and the air seemed to change.

'I don't think you should kiss this one,' Madonna said.

'No?'

She shook her head.

'Do you see any lipstick? People mostly cry over it. Not kiss it.'

'All right. Wouldn't want to break any rules or anything,' I said in a low voice.

There they were. Lying side by side, in stone. A monk and a nun. They seemed like just about any other couple asleep on a bed, only they didn't have their arms around one another, they were posed with their hands in prayer.

'Do you know when this tomb was made?' I asked.

'About 1817, I think.'

I turned to Madonna.

'654 years after they died?

She shrugged her shoulders.

'I guess so. Their bones were preserved. A very powerful story, no? Their bones protected, saved, all that time.'

'They must have wanted to hold on to some proof of the myth.'

'Yes. Love is a powerful myth.'

This seemed like a very cogent thing for a man living as Madonna to say.

'Like religion,' I said. 'People want very much to believe in it.'

I took pictures as we talked of many things people believed then and now.

'Love is always a part of it.'

'Do you believe in it, Madonna? In the myth of love?'

She clasped her hands together, the long, painted nails fell into a swirl of color around her hands.

'But of course! I have been in love many times! It's wonderful! What would the world be without love?'

I nodded.

'That's great. It's true. Love is quite an adventure.'

'So, you've found love then, Grant?'

For all the intimate details I was asking for about these actors, I felt a curious reserve myself. My thoughts of my wife were my own. Yet, how could I expect Madonna to share with me if I was unwilling to do the same?

'Katie saved me. Eight years ago, when I stumbled onto her doorstep in a rainstorm.' The thought of it made me blush still. How lost I was. In so many ways.

'Ahhh! Rescued by your woman. That explains your romantic nature, Grant.'

'Yes, I suppose so. We have a daughter too. Ariel.'

'Show me.'

I pulled out my phone and produced the 600 or so pictures I had of Ariel and Katie. Then I showed her our nautical themed wedding on the beach of St. Ives. She seemed unsurprised by this. As if such weddings were the norm.

'Who is the lobster?'

'That's my dad. He's a professor at USC in California. I never thought he'd come.'

'And the mermaid is Katie?'

'Yes.'

'She's beautiful.'

'She is.'

'What are you supposed to be? I don't understand.'

'I'm Aquaman! There's my trident!'

'Ohhhhh! I see now. Very...sexy this Aquaman of the sea.'

'Thanks.'

'Now, we go to another of the famous cemeteries. More lovely things for you to take pictures of.'

I felt extremely lucky to have Madonna as my guide. I'd never find these places on my own.

~

At the Montmartre Cemetery we found the tomb of Edgar Degas, the impressionist. One of my favorite artists. The inscription was something of an understatement. 'He loved to draw very much.' It was undeniable that there was something palpable about standing near the ground that held the bones of this artist who so beautifully captured life. It was entirely different to being under the ground with the bones of masses of people I didn't know anything about. That experience felt suffocating and frightening, like death itself. This one made me feel a connection to a man who made such an effort to communicate something about humanity.

Still, all this death made me ache for my wife – the woman I associated with life. It made me remember that my path toward who I really was had only started when I met her. It was only then that it dawned on me that I could have the work I dreamed of. I could *be* a photographer. Katie had done this. She'd seen my photographs and not only thought it possible but thought it essential that I change professions.

In less than a week she'd got me a settlement from my contract with my old boss (she was a great lawyer), introduced me to Leslie, and got me the visa I needed to stay and see what might happen between us. It didn't take six months. I knew I'd found her, the person I belonged with. I am grateful every day that she said yes. Life with Katie has been an adventure.

Madonna and I walked around in silence for a while. This is what cemeteries do to you. You become the silence. At around six in the evening, Madonna looked at her watch and said she had to go home. I thanked her for spending the day with me. I walked her to the metro, and she kissed both my cheeks and said goodbye.

'Bonne nuit, mon Chéri, fais de beaux rêves.'

When I looked confused, she translated for me.

'Good night, dear. Sweet dreams!

Chapter Eight

That night, I was on the phone with my daughter, and she grilled me about my new friends.

'But how do you talk to them if you don't speak French?'

'They speak a bit of English and I bring my dictionary. It's hard, but not impossible. We have fun. You can do that in any language.'

'So, you play together?'

'Yes, that's exactly what we do. And they let me take their pictures while we play.'

'Oh, good. I want to see them.'

'You will. And I think you'll like them.'

'When will you be home, Daddy? I miss you.'

'Not long now. In about ten days.'

'All right. Mum wants to say goodbye.'

'OK. Put her on then. Goodnight sweetheart. Love you.'

'Love you too. Here's Mum.'

'Hi. Doing anything fun for Bastille Day?'

'Yes. Meeting my new friends at the old Menagerie. They said it's their favorite place.'

She made one of her noises. Like a low growl.

'What?'

'I hope they're all right. They sound a little...'

'Touched?'

'Yes. A bit.'

'They're hard to explain, dear, but there's really something quite ... I don't know ... innocent ... and playful about them. I've come to like them a lot.'

She sighed.

'You've told me about LA crazy versus New York crazy.'

'Yeah.' New York crazies, I'd told Katie, just wanted money. LA crazies wanted to hurt you for entertainment. 'These are Paris crazies and I think they just want to be themselves. They aren't trying to rob me or anything. In fact, they've been generous with the only thing they have, which is time.'

'Well, your time is limited. Are they keeping you from your work?'

'Not at all. In fact, I find amazing pictures in their company. They show me things I like. I've been lucky to find them.'

'All right then. If you're happy, I'm happy.'

~

On Bastille Day, July 14th, I went to meet my Paris crazy friends at the Menagerie. It was a very small zoo at the Jardin des Plantes. On my way in I was reading a bit of Wiki history about the zoo on my phone. Originally the animals were brought into the gardens from the King's palace at Versailles in 1794, but because of the revolution, the zoo was abandoned and left to the scientists to manage. It was very clear that nothing much had been done with it after a while. It was a few old buildings containing some rare species of birds and reptiles. I wandered around until I came to the cage that now held one lion. It was a heart-breaking sight. It gazed out at me through the rusted iron bars.

The cage was about the size of Héloïse and Abélard's tomb. The lion was laying on the ground, two golden eyes watching my every move. As I took pictures, and after I finished, I heard the cries of my friends behind me, and turned. They lowered their voices as they approached.

'It is sad, our friend in this cage, is it not?' asked Bear. 'But he remains beautiful. Strong.'

'Yes,' I said. In truth there just weren't any words to describe the feeling. A strange mix of humility and shame. It wasn't right to have such a proud animal entrapped like this. Perhaps not right to have any animal in a cage. I was glad zoos like this, with cages and bars, had gone out of fashion in the late 19th century. Bear told us this was one of the last ones remaining in Paris.

'We call him Leo,' said Joan. She then called his name and approached the cage. He stood up and pressed his head against the bars as if to answer her.

'Careful...' I said.

'Leo knows me. He's not afraid.'

'No?'

'Non.'

I took a few pictures of Leo, and he sat back down again.

'You may never get to be this close to a lion again in your life,' said Bear. He was staring longingly at Leo. 'He's magnificent.'

'How long do you think they'll keep him like this?'

'Not much longer. I think they are looking for a new home for him in a modern zoo. No cages. When they find one, they will no longer have a lion here and will take down this cage.'

I couldn't take my eyes off this lion. His glittering orbs sparkled with intelligence. He was just as curious about us as we were about him. Then Bear rolled around on the ground and pretended to be a lion.

Leo blinked and stood up, a bit alarmed by this behavior.

All of us involuntarily took a step back and watched the lion. Bear was frozen and didn't move. And then Leo opened his mouth and roared! For a thundering few seconds! My hair must have been standing up as we slowly, noiselessly, walked away from the cage together. We broke into a laugh to ease the tension. We walked around a bit more, but the other buildings were closed.

'I have an idea!' said JC. 'I want to show you all something. A place we've not been to together before. It isn't far.'

'Does it follow the guidelines?' asked Bear.

'What guidelines?' I asked.

'It must stimulate our senses somehow. That's our rule when we go on adventures together. We must feel something out of the ordinary.'

'Oh, oui! It is both sight and smell and you will love it!' she said.

'Then lead on!' Madonna cried.

We followed JC, two by two, on the pavement. I walked next to Joan.

'Bear likes it when our little trips make us feel alive,' she explained.

'I do too. Not the usual tourist sights,' I said.

'We live on love and the senses, like the artists here have always done. Being poor makes us use our brains more and we seek out the things we might not otherwise notice.'

'That's why I am so lucky to have met you. I feel that's why I came here. To see Paris like an artist here might see it.'

This made Joan smile.

We came to a stop in front of a flower shop. The name painted on the front read: La Vie en Rose. It was a very small shop. JC gathered us together in a circle.

'There are too many of us to all go in at the same time. Find a partner. We'll go in twos.'

Bruce Lee was scratching his head.

'A flower shop? Really? This is your sensory experience for us?'

JC straightened her back and gave him a cold stare.

'Dr. Freud? You will come with me. The rest of you, choose your partner and wait your turn. We will have about ten minutes in there and then we will come back out. Agreed?'

We all agreed. Madonna took my arm. The mime and statue stood together behind us. Bear and Joan stood behind them, and Bruce was last.

'Hey look! A crêperie!' Bear was pointing to a place across the street. 'You all go ahead of us, and Joan and I can get us all some lunch. What do you want?'

'Nutella and banana,' Madonna said. 'Ditto for me,' I said. I could never have enough of those.

'I'll have mushroom and onion,' Bruce said. 'Get JC and the doctor the same. I know they like those.'

When Dr. Freud came out with JC, her face was beaming, and tears were streaming down her cheeks. She trembled as she wiped her face with a handkerchief.

'Are you alright?' asked Madonna, stroking Dr. Freud's arm.

Dr. Freud nodded as she cried harder.

I wondered what on earth had happened in there. JC was weeping too.

'A lot of beauty in there. Go on. You two are next.'

She waved us in, and Joan and I took a deep breath and stepped over the threshold of the little flower shop.

The smell came first. Hitting me like a tsunami of olfactory bliss. An intense aroma of citrus and cloves and other spices and scents. Perfumed perfection. Then there was the sight of them. Roses. Big. Glorious. Overflowing. Buckets of them. All arranged by color, from slight variations of white, cream, yellow, pale pink, then deep pink, red and orange. The shop was filled with them. Long stem. Cut. It was like we had stepped into rose heaven.

I couldn't guess how many roses were in there were. It seemed like thousands. These were not small buds but huge, the size of a coffee cup! And they were all close together in bundles. That wonderful photograph of just four roses, by Tina Modotti, a Mexican photographer, popped into my head. So sensual, the composition was at once familiar and new. She had them close together and leaning against one another, almost like a family, just like this.

JC was right. It was an emotional experience of the senses. My eyes were overloading on the sights and my nostrils were flexing with the aroma all around me. Just as the croissants had flooded my brain and brought on memories, this room made me see hundreds of images in my mind of my favorite experiences of roses, from my grandmother's garden to ones I had visited around the world, in pictures, story and song. Some of my favorite people had rose gardens.

Madonna had her hands out like she was flying, and her eyes were closed. Her fingers were touching the tops of the roses and she was heaving big sobs from her chest. It struck me that she was undergoing something even more intense than I was and that perhaps I should get her out of here, but then, who was I to interrupt her revelation? Perhaps she didn't want it to end.

I swept my camera over them, snapping pictures that I knew would never do justice to this experience. But the failure wasn't important. You carried something of the memory of every attempt you made to take a picture. This was what photography was about. The attempt to capture a shared human experience. To capture time and memory itself.

This indoor field of roses was having a profound effect on me, a city boy. I don't recall ever seeing a huge gathering of roses growing up, but it was like I was *remembering* this sea of roses. Was it in a past life? I turned my head to see Madonna. Her eyes blinked open. What, I wondered, was *she* remembering?

Sometime later, we stumbled out of the shop together, Madonna holding my hand as if for dear life. JC put her arms around her and rocked her like a child. She kissed the top of her head. I wanted to ask her what had happened, what it had been like for her, but sensed she wasn't ready to talk about it yet.

Bruce ran in to have his turn while the rest of us waited for Bear and Joan. When they came back with the food, we all busied ourselves with eating rather than explaining our experience. There was a deep joy going around though, a profound satisfaction. We finished our meal and watched in anticipation as Bear and Joan went in.

Ten minutes went by, but they didn't come out. We waited another ten minutes.

'Shall I go get them?' I offered.

'Non. We wait a bit longer,' JC said.

We waited. Finally, Joan came out. Eyes wide. She was alone.

'Where's Bear?' Bruce asked.

'You won't believe it. You won't believe it.'

'What?' Madonna said. 'Where is he?'

'He's got himself a new job in there!' Joan laughed.

'He did?' JC was the most surprised of all of us.

'Oui. He didn't move or say anything for ten minutes and then he asked to see the owner and they went out the back and talked. When he came back, he was shaking hands with him.'

Bear appeared in the doorway with the biggest smile on his face.

'I have a new calling.'

He went straight up to JC and hugged her.

'Thank you,' he said. 'I owe you one.'

Jesus wept.

Chapter Nine

It turns out that Bear did indeed have a transformative vision when he saw the roses in the flower shop. He said it all came together for him at once. Being a bouncer for the HIDE was not the job of his dreams but delivering roses for La Vie en Rose was. He got along famously with the owner. Best boss he ever had. We didn't see Bear much during the day anymore. He worked from six in the morning until around four in the afternoon.

Tonight, we were all together at the HIDE having drinks. He looked happy. And I noticed he kept staring at Joan. Dreamy eyed. I suspected they had a thing going. I was showing them all the photos I'd managed to take in the three weeks I'd been in Paris. I'd got a contact sheet made at a photography store of some of the best pictures on my digital camera. There were over three hundred images that I kept. It included the tarnished gentlemen from the Gard du Nord, a frowning Mrs. Garnier, models, glaring at me on the Champs-Élysées. There were many patisseries, the Seine in rain and sun and at different times of day, the policeman who told me off. The priest walking down the street looked interesting next to the lion at the Menagerie. The roses at the La Vie en Rose were there, the store fronts at the Île de Saint-Louise and Île de la Citié. My portrait of Indigo, the pirate king, on his bicycle stood out. So young and fierce. But it was the photos of my new friends that filled me with the most pride. I watched their faces as they recognized each other.

Joan touched the one of her, standing on the rock wall in the piazza. Her fists were raised, her eyes locked on someone in the crowd. Her message urgent and inspired. I had pictures of people watching her too. Some were right there with her, arms raised in solidarity. Fight the English! Others had a weary expression. Some were puzzled by the timing of her speech. Others were delighted. She was entertaining them. Then there were the pictures I took of her when she was relaxing with us, that first pizza lunch we shared. I was able to catch her untroubled, laughing even. A young Joan of Arc at play. Now I noticed that in that picture Bear was watching her the same way he watched her still, with love and devotion.

Statue looked like a statue. Nothing much revealed. I did get one moment of him taking off his make-up, in which he spotted my camera and scowled at me. Was this why he always seemed mad? I couldn't crack the surface of this man's steely heart.

Marcel seemed born for the camera. Every shot of him was perfect. Clear. Sharp. I understood now that there was much more going on with Marcel than you might notice with the eye. The camera captured a very complex series of moves, all practiced to perfection. He was a magician who could draw people into his silent stories. I had a great image of him striking the pose of Rodin's famous statue, *The Thinker*.

Bruce darted around a lot. Most of his pictures were blurry, but that's because I wanted to show that sense of motion about him. It was Bruce who was hardest to know. Even harder than Statue. At least Statue was clear that he didn't want to be known. But Bruce was always with us, but seldom revealed himself. Sometimes he did combat scenes with Marcel. At the Pompidou, he did martial arts demonstrations and even signed autographs as Bruce Lee, for kids. They loved him. But no matter how many pictures I took of Bruce, he wasn't really *there*.

Madonna, like Marcel, was photogenic. She had winning smiles for everyone even though some people were clearly confused by her. Most were appreciative of her voice though, and her dance moves. She was a professional performer and it showed in the pictures.

Dr. Freud, with her brown suit, waistcoat, and round glasses, was something out of a different time. She didn't look anything like the man, but in her quiet way, she practiced the profession. The photographs I took of her, deep in conversation with those seated at her desk, showed she had real compassion for her 'patients.' She may have been a performer, but she was really listening to people who told her their problems.

The woman who called herself JC was hard to capture. She was camera shy, always ducking away from me any time she noticed my camera. She would put her hands up and walk away. I only had a few candid shots of her.

'You went against her wishes,' said Statue.

'All right, all right. Look. I'll delete them. Will that make you happy?' I asked her.

'Yes.'

I hesitated.

'I really want to remember you. And having a picture helps.'

'Are you going to respect her wishes or not?' said Statue, who then knocked back another gin.

I could see she was suffering, so I deleted them. Painful as it was.

'There. It's done.'

'I'm sorry,' she said. 'But you'll remember me. I promise.' Then she smiled.

She was right. I would.

'So, you're going to leave us soon, eh?' Bear asked. He'd been paying attention.

All faces turned to me.

'Yeah, Friday is my last day in Paris. My plane leaves that evening.'

'Ohhhh, Grant. We're going to miss you, darling,' Madonna said.

'Yes, you are my favorite Englishman.' Joan smiled, raising her glass.

I blinked. This surprised me.

'Really?'

'Really.'

'We should all do something together for your last day,' Bear said.

'I'd like that. In fact, I have something I'd like to propose.'

They all leaned forward a little. 'I'm grateful for the pictures you've let me take. You've helped me improve my portfolio. I've learned a lot on this trip and much of that is because of you guys.' I looked directly at Madonna. 'You've been so kind. I'd like to take you all to a place I've been saving for my last day. Would you please come with me to the Louvre? Just for the afternoon. On Friday. I'll pay for everyone's ticket. It will be fun.'

Statue put his head on the table and moaned, then jumped as Bear kicked him.

'Course we can,' Bear said. His face set in a smile.

Marcel did a fluttery silent clapping motion with his hands. His face registered something between pure excitement and horror.

'You want us to take a Friday afternoon off? From our work?' Statue said.

I swallowed. It *was* asking a lot.

'My boss said she wanted to do a piece on my trip to Paris. She might publish these pictures in the magazine. *Cornwall Today.*' Statue snorted. 'I'd just like to take a few more of you and we might have fun together there.'

'I've got better things to–hey!' Statue doubled over as Bear punched him in the arm.

'Thank you, Grant,' Bear said. 'We'd all be happy to go to the Louvre with you on Friday afternoon. No problem.' Bear smiled at Joan, and she was beaming.

'It's very sweet of you,' Madonna crooned. She blew me a kiss. 'You are a doll. I can't wait!'

'Me too!' Joan cried.

'I've never been to the Louvre.' Bruce said. 'Might be fun.'

'I have an idea,' Dr. Freud said. 'We can each pick one painting or sculpture that is our favorite and share why that is.'

Everyone, including me, seemed a bit stunned by this idea, but I could see they were all thinking about it.

'We could do that,' Bear said. 'Right, Statue?'

Statue raised his angry head, narrowed his bloodshot eyes at me and said, 'Oui, con.'

Chapter Ten

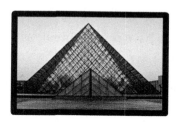

On Friday morning I got myself packed and decided with Madame Garnier to leave the keys with her and pick up my stuff on the way to the airport. I'd take a taxi from the Louvre and head on to the airport. I made a quick call to Katie, checking in with her.

'So, you got your pictures then?' she said.

'I think so. A lot of them, anyway. I'll edit them when I get back. I like the look of some of them.'

'Sounds like you met some interesting people.'

'I was lucky, really. That they took me in.'

I could feel her smiling over the phone.

'You attract interesting people.'

'Well, it will be nice to get home. Kiss Ariel for me. I miss her to pieces. And you too.'

'Thanks, dear. Have you picked up any French?'

'Oui! Buckets of it!'

She laughed, which filled my cup for the day. Everything would go perfectly. I was sure of it.

As I came out of the flat complex, I saw the crêpe place and walked over to have my last breakfast in Paris.

'Bonjour, Marie!' I said, breezily.

The day was warm already, at nine-thirty. The sun was beating down through a cloudless sky.

'Bonjour, Grant!' she said back to me, with a shy smile. Marie and I had formed habits in the four weeks I had been here. She was always busy with her hands, putting something away, cleaning a spot on the counter, checking the heat on the griddle. Every day she wore a clean apron over a gathered skirt and a top with long sleeves. Her round face was always hot, glistening with sweat.

'What shall I have today?' I always asked, like a man of means and adventure.

Here, she would also pretend that she was offering me the world. She raised her arm to the menu behind her. There must have been a hundred variations on sweet and savory crêpes.

'Sweet or savory?' she would say.

'Oh, what the heck. Today is my last day. How about sweet.'

She blinked at me. This was not her usual response.

'You go home?'

'That's right. Tonight. Going to the Louvre today. Then to the airport.'

She gave a deep sigh.

'Then you must have the special, Grant. Remember, you haven't had it yet. You wanted to save it, for later.'

'Right. As I recall, it looked decadent.'

She giggled. Her tiny hand went up to her mouth and covered her smile.

'Nutella and banana.'

'Oh my.'

'Yes. Very good. And for you, extra Nutella, Grant.'

Now I was giggling like a goose.

'Really?'

'Just for you. I like you, Grant. I will miss you.'

And for a moment, she looked into my eyes, and I saw hers were sad. That I might cheer her up a little in her daily work, where she stood making crêpes all day long, had never occurred to me.

'Why thank you, Marie. I will miss you too.' Then I held up my camera. 'I'm a photographer. May I take your picture?'

She glanced around, as if checking that no one would see her smile. Then she grinned and nodded as she poured the batter on the griddle and took her little wooden stick and twirled it around to spread the batter.

I took a dozen pictures of her doing her art, for Marie did her work with love and precision. The smell of the batter cooking and the click of my shutter reminded me that I was here, now, in Paris, having a moment of full living.

She slathered Nutella on the warm disc then sliced a banana and arranged it on top with her blue latex gloved hands. Then she folded and wrapped it in the way she had practiced, thousands of times. She smiled as she presented it to me.

'I hope you have had a good time here.'

'Oh, I shall never forget it.' I bit into the crêpe, and it was insanely good. She laughed at me as I moaned in pleasure and watched me down the whole thing. When I had wiped my lips and fingers and deposited the paper plate and napkin in the trash, she extended her hand to me over the counter. I took both her hands in mine and bowed.

'Thank you, Marie. You have started my every morning here with joy and nourishment. I appreciate seeing your smile every day too.'

She nodded and pulled her hand away as another customer approached. I took my leave but heard her call after me.

'Goodbye, Grant! It was a pleasure to see your face every day.'

I ambled down the Seine toward the Latin Quarter. There were a few hours left for me to explore and I'd been told there was a place that had once been a Roman arena. It took me a while to find it, but when I did, it was surprising. The place seemed to have been completely forgotten. No signs or guides, no tickets to pay to see it. There was a little plaque with some information and a stone seating arrangement with nothing but lifeless, dusty dirt in the ringed center. It stood between forlorn, sagging flat buildings as if it were a deserted disco club, or some other failed commercial enterprise of decades past, not the archeological evidence of Roman occupation in 259 BC! As big as a football field, one could imagine gladiators fighting bears, lions, and each other. There were animal enclosures facing the arena. The ghostly feeling of people long dead drifted around the place and reminded me of my visit to the catacombs. Again, curiously, it was interesting, but I had no impulse to take pictures of it. My subject was life, not history, not death. I decided to head off to find some lunch.

I'd read something online about a mosque near here that had a restaurant inside and was curious to see what it was like, so I consulted my map and headed that way. It was not hard to spot. A smooth white wall enclosed other buildings of a similar style and stood out from everything else. When I walked through the archway, everything changed. I effectively left Paris and stepped into a spiritual sanctuary, a place of peace.

The energy of the place was completely different than from the Roman arena where I had just been. Here was an interior garden carefully arranged, with plants that offered shade and delight. Blue and white tiles with intricate designs decorated the ground. Outdoor chairs and tables offered visitors a rest. An oasis. I found the entrance to the restaurant and entered, immediately enveloped in deep reds, oranges and blues of geometric paintings and fabrics. It was as if I'd entered a womb. The walls and furniture converged to meet and hold me in luxurious hospitality. The smell of the delicious middle eastern food and pastries were all around me along with the faint aroma of honey, mint, and lemon. This experience was something to take in with my senses, not my camera. A man dressed in a simple Abaya greeted me in a friendly manner and took me to a table where I was seated and given a menu.

I ordered something called Brique au Thon, which turned out to be a brick of tuna fish, kind of like a fish stick or fish finger in English, but instead of being wrapped in batter it was wrapped in a pastry. I liked it. Then I ordered some sweet pastries. The Corne de gazelle blanche, which translates as White Gazelle Horn, was a powdered sugar dusted cookie shaped like a crescent moon. I had some fresh mint tea with my Baklava cigar and felt like a Sultan. It was all very exotic to me, a rare treat. After having my fill of tea and earthly delights, I headed out to continue my wandering way.

Walking toward the Louvre where I was to meet my friends, I reviewed the time I'd spent in Paris thus far. I'd steered clear of museums because I wanted to explore Paris in my own way, not by spending whole days in buildings. After my initial experience of being robbed, the experience of walking and riding the metro all over gave me a sense of the size and variety of the different neighborhoods and cultures in Paris and I was enjoying seeing as many of those places as I could.

But now, the pull of the Louvre was strong. Art had always been important to me. As a rather aloof teenager, I instructed my parents to drop me off at the Los Angeles Museum of Art on the first Saturday of each month. My mother took me there at ten in the morning and picked me up at four in the afternoon. I loved my time alone there. Every painting had something to say to me. And I listened, going from one to the other, stopping only to eat a sandwich at lunchtime.

Later, when I studied at an art school in downtown Los Angeles on weekends, I stretched canvases, and painted from live models. Gradually, painting had to give way to photography, and I put my brushes away. But now that I was here, the pull of the Louvre made me long to see those paintings I'd always loved but never stood in front of.

At one o'clock I was at the glass pyramid entrance where I found my performer friends. There was a long line, but we took our place in it. I had tickets for everyone. Statue was in full make up, obviously intending to work today. I could hardly blame him. There were a lot of people here. And they stared at him. He stood there licking an ice cream cone. An odd sight. I couldn't resist snapping pictures with my lucky Nikon.

Statue took a long lick as he noticed me photographing him, his eyes radiating disgust. For a moment I thought of Robert Doisneau and tried to draw inspiration from that photographer, his way of capturing children in those moments of innocent pleasure. With his hard metal face, Statue looked more like a demon than an innocent, but there was something beneath the surface, a childish, single-minded determination to enjoy that ice cream, no matter what.

When I put my camera down, JC approached me and spoke in a low voice. 'I'm not coming in with you,' she said, lowering her head. Despite her soft voice, everyone in our little group heard her and turned to face her.

'What do you mean?' I asked, perplexed.

'I'm just here to say good-bye. You're leaving to go home when the museum closes, around five, right? She pushed her sunglasses back on her head and threw her skinny arms around my neck. She smelled of bread and cut grass. She whispered in my ear. 'It's been a pleasure, Grant. I wish you every success with your photographs.'

'I wish you would reconsider,' I said back to her. She lowered her eyes as she gently pulled back, tucking her hair behind her ears.

'I can't go in there.' She winced. 'Too many crucifixions. Depressing.'

I could see her point.

'All right then. I'm just sorry not to have a bit more time with you.' And I meant it. She was an odd one, but I liked her.

'Could I please take just one picture of you? To remember you by?'

She nodded, lowering her sunglasses. I found her in the viewfinder, beside the glass pyramid. Jesus, the tourist, and snapped the picture.

'Have fun,' she called out to us.

As we watched her trot away, I heard Statue say, ominously, 'And then there were eight.'

An hour later we were finally through the ticket line on the ground floor. We came to an indoor courtyard, covered in glass, where there was a marble block with four bronze statues of soldiers, each one chained to a corner. It was called *Four Captives*.

Statue spread his arms wide.

'My people!' he cried as he stepped over the thin metal guard rail, climbed the block, and stood next to one of the captives. 'This,' he said, smiling over at me, 'is my favorite art piece. I can relate, for I too am a captive.' He had his hand on his chest and a wide grin as he watched my reaction.

'Ha ha,' Bear said. 'Get down from there, before you get us in trouble.'

Dr. Freud walked over to where he was standing and read from the brochure.

'Each soldier expresses a different reaction to captivity: revolt, hope, resignation, grief.' She pushed her glasses up her nose and asked, 'which aspect are you?'

'Bored!' he yelled at her. Luckily, we were the only ones in the courtyard. He pulled a cloth cap out of his pocket and placed it by his foot on the stone block, sat down, and took his position next to the captive. In a matter of moments,

138

before our eyes, he turned into the fifth bronze captive. I had to admire the man's talent. He fit right in. And I took his portrait, among his people.

'Let's go,' Bear said. 'I don't think anyone will notice him.'

Bear led the way and we all followed, heading toward the stairs.

'And then there were seven!' Statue called after us.

'We'll pick you up on our way out!' I called back over my shoulder.

Madonna took my arm and walked beside me.

'Don't take it personally. He gets a bit overwhelmed by crowds. This is how he makes himself feel safe. By being invisible.'

I stopped and stared at her. It made sense, what she said. She took the map from me, then studied it. 'I'd like to see *Winged Victory*. On the next floor up. Can we go there first?'

Everyone was agreeable and we climbed the stairs to the Denon Wing. The Daru staircase. When she saw it, Madonna clasped her hands together. Her mouth curled up at the corners. Her eyes were dancing with excitement. I thought she might burst into song.

'Magnifique,' she whispered, and took a step closer. We all took up a position near the eighteen-foot-high statue and gaped. Headless. Armless. Blind and powerless. It was blindingly beautiful with those magnificent wings carved from stone. Another elegant, and poetic contradiction.

'How did this guy make something look so soft out of stone? Look at the feathers! The drapery!' Bear said.

Bruce crossed his arms as he read out the description. 'Found in 1863 by Charles Champoiseau. It is believed to be the Greek God Nike, who personified victory and was erected as part of the Sanctuary of the Great Gods on the island of Samothrace.'

'Vic-tor-y,' Madonna said in one long breath.

I got her to stand at the base of the sculpture while I went to the ground with my camera and aimed up, so it looked like the wings were behind her. Madonna the angel.

Bear rubbed his eyes, still unable to believe the craftsmanship.

'Serious skill,' he said.

'It's beautiful,' Joan said. Then turning to Madonna, she said, 'Like you.'

Madonna looked at Joan then, a little glassy eyed. An invisible yet palpable wave of gratitude travelled from Madonna and landed on Joan, who gave a soft nod of her head.

'It's the wings I like best,' Madonna said, continuing with her revelry. She sniffled as she took a napkin out of her pocket and wiped her eyes. 'She's my guardian angel. Watches out for me in a cruel world.' She accidently rubbed a bit of mascara off her eye, appearing in that moment so vulnerable that I held my breath as I watched her. When we finally walked on, I was beside her and took her arm.

'You've seen Nike here before, haven't you?'

'Well, of course, Chéri. I visit her whenever I can.'

Bruce's face screwed up and he stiffened as he turned toward her, his eyebrows at odds.

'You've been coming here? To the Louvre?'

'Oui. Sometimes. I have a pass.'

'You never said.'

'You don't know everything about me, do you?'

'Apparently not.'

'Have you never been here, Darling?' Her voice was gentle with him. Sympathetic.

Bruce rolled his eyes and went on to the next painting. It seemed he had not and was a bit embarrassed by this. She turned to me.

'Did you study art in school, Grant?'

'I used to teach art and photography. In California.'

They all turned to me and stopped walking. A little circle of incredulity.

'In a school?' Bear asked.

'Oui.' I said, standing a little taller. 'A *fancy* one. In Los Angeles. But that was a long time ago.'

'Oh, I see. So, this is why you thought it would be fun to bring us all here,' Bear said. I noticed Joan elbowed him in the ribs.

'Let's keep moving.' Bruce took the lead now and we all followed. He looked like a Chinese Emperor, hands clasped behind his back, strolling along on the red carpets of this century's old palace.

I was enjoying the conversations we were having about art, but at the same time, getting more uncomfortable with all the heavy security here. Without doubt we were being monitored. Cameras were everywhere. Uniformed guards at every door, highly alert to possible attacks on the art. It was like airport security. No one had a sense of humor.

We made our way to the seven hundred gallery, where we found French paintings. High ceilings. Red walls. Everyone's eyes were wide as we all turned and scanned the room. Bear stopped in his tracks and then headed straight for one painting. We noticed his engagement and followed. It was Delacroix's painting of two tigers. One the mother of the other.

'This is mine,' he said in reverence. Joan came and stood beside him, then took his hand in hers. Bear didn't need any signs. His eyes told him everything he needed to know.

Dr. Freud came up close to him as she gazed at the painting. 'Even behind bars, these tigers are majestic.'

I asked Bear if I could photograph him beside this painting and he nodded. He and Joan turned around and stood there, unsmiling. As cool and distant as the tigers.

'She sees us,' Bear said to me. For a moment I thought he meant Dr. Freud, but then realized he meant the tigress.

'Yes. She's regarding us humans,' I said.

'And we don't come off well,' he answered. 'She is not impressed.'

'Non.'

I had to hand it to Delacroix. The tigress was portrayed with deep knowledge. It was incredible. How did he know the tiger like this? Had he seen one in the wild? This animal reminded me of the caged lion. At least that lion would die at some point and so escape his captivity. But Delacroix had fixed this tigress in paint, to live forever free and wild. This was something I could see was hugely important to Bear.

The wildness *and* the freedom.

Chapter Eleven

When we were all gathered again and ready to move on, we came to a large crowd ahead of us. People had cell phones and cameras raised above their heads, as if a celebrity had arrived.

'What's going on?' Bruce asked a man near us.

'It's the Mona Lisa. Bit of a bottleneck.'

'I've seen pictures of that one,' Bruce said. He turned to the rest of us. 'Let's give it a pass,'

Everyone else in our little group followed Bruce, but I didn't move. Was he kidding? Maybe it didn't matter much to them, but I'd seen pictures of that painting all my life and now that I was here, how could I *not* see the Mona Lisa?

'Wait!' They stopped and faced me. 'Couldn't we at least peek? Long as we're here?' I sounded like a kid asking my parents.

Bruce squinted at me. Like a fed-up parent.

Bear clenched his teeth and snarled.

Joan blinked. I'm not sure she understood the situation at all.

Marcel stared at the ceiling, getting other people to look up.

Dr. Freud wet her lips.

'Of course, we can,' Madonna snapped at them.

We all took our place in this new line and passed the time trying to guess what animal Marcel was trying to be as I took pictures. Snap, snap, snap. A satisfying sound. He almost exploded doing a blowfish. We were entertained.

When we finally had our turn to see the great lady, we stood before a table, or maybe it was an altar. The painting was dimly lit and behind glass. It was disappointingly small.

'Ok,' I said. 'On the count of three, put your thumb up if you like it, or down if you don't. Don't think about it. Just how you feel. Ready? One, two, THREE!'

Madonna, Joan, and Dr. Freud had their thumbs up. Bear, Bruce, and Marcel had thumbs down. I stood there. No thumbs.

'What about you, art teacher?' Bear demanded.

'I can't possibly decide. It's a tie.'

'Is this how you taught art? Thumbs up or thumbs down?' Bruce barked.

Marcel seemed to speak for everyone when he slapped his cheeks and pulled the face like in the painting called 'The Scream' by Edvard Munch.

'No way,' Bear said, his hand on my shoulder. 'You have to vote, man. We all did it.'

'Let's not argue.'

'We want to know your vote!' he yelled. Everyone in line turned around to look at him.

'Shhhh!' I tried to bring Bear back into line and quiet him down. It was obvious he was upsetting people. Embarrassing me. I wondered if this whole idea had been a bad one.

A big man with baggy eyes, who was behind us, tapped my shoulder. When I turned around, he put out his large chin and said, in a Texas drawl, 'Are you idiot? People don't pay good money and line up here for hours to see a bad painting. The experts of the world, the ones who know something about this, think it's good. You might at least try and learn something. Take your lousy opinions and get out of the way! Some of us would like to see it. Quietly.'

I herded my friends out of the gallery.

Chapter Twelve

Madonna started to giggle when we got to the next room.

'That wasn't funny!' Bruce said and turned to me, his face crimson. 'No more thumbs up or thumbs down, Grant!' I'd never seen Bruce so mad.

'I'm sorry, OK? I was just curious about how everyone else felt. I never could decide if I liked it or not and being up close didn't sway me one way or the other.'

'Well, I think that's the genius of it,' Dr. Freud said. 'It's art that's got the power to reveal something about the viewer. Like a ... a ... what do you call it in English, Grant? The test with ink blots?'

'A Rorschach test?'

'Yes. Inkblots.'

I glanced at my phone. Not much longer before we'd have to go. We came to more French paintings. I liked these works. Nothing unclear about them. They were not vague. They were mysterious and stirring, but you knew what you were looking at. There was a plot to these paintings. Like *The Raft of the Medusa* by Théodore Géricault. Desperation, fear, hope expressed so well in each body on that raft, even with their backs to us! I then heard Joan's voice and turned around. *What now?*

'*Liberté*!' Joan cried, her arms up like she was greeting a long lost relative. Bear, standing next to her, beckoned us with both fleshy hands. We quickened our pace towards them and stopped in front of *Liberty Leading the People* by Delacroix. I glanced over at Dr. Freud. We were in complete agreement. How could this not be Joan's favorite? Yet, Joan seemed completely surprised to see it here.

'Have you not seen this painting before?' I asked her. Well, I suppose Joan of Arc wouldn't have.

'Non! It is magnifique!'

Boy, she was good.

'Your favorite then?'

'Oui! Oui!' She was so full of joy, she hopped from one foot to the other. Her eyes never left the canvas. Both her hands were balled into tight little fists of excitement. Bear was basking in her happiness, his face radiating contentment.

'She is so strong,' whispered Joan. 'She doesn't feel the cold.'

'May I take your picture with it?' I asked.

'Oui!'

She combed her hair with her fingers and spun around, grinning. Great shot.

Dr. Freud cleared her throat.

'*Liberté* could use more clothes,' she muttered to me under her breath. After consulting her watch, Dr. Freud pushed her glasses up her nose again, cleared her throat.

'The Louvre closes very soon. They start clearing the rooms at five and are very serious about getting people out. Could we go to the next level up? I'd like to show you my favorite painting. In the Sully Room.'

I turned to Dr. Freud. 'You know exactly what room your favorite painting is in?'

She nodded once. All business, that one. She had clearly been here before too.

We made our way up the staircase as everyone else was going down. When we reached the next gallery, it was ten minutes to five. We were walking through it when I heard Bruce calling for everyone to halt. That got my attention.

'This one's mine,' he said with a big smile on his face. He stood before a dark oil painting of modest size, about five feet by three feet. We gathered around him and the painting. *Seaport by Moonlight*. The painter was Claude Joseph Vernet. A peaceful sea reflected the moon. People were gathered around a fire, their faces glowing in an orange light. You could almost hear the groaning of the ships as they gently rocked back and forth on the water, and the crackling of the wood on the fire.

'I know this place, even though I've never been here,' Bruce said, surprising us all. This man of few words seemed to be *travelling* into this painting. With unblinking eyes, he leaned forward, mouth slack. It was calling to him, as if from another time, another life. And he was going. Slipping away from us.

'It's nicely done,' Bear said, as if to break the spell and bring him back.

'Beautiful,' Madonna whispered, a little starry eyed.

'There is such peace in it,' Joan marveled, the woman of war.

Marcel just rocked back and forth as if with the splash of the waves on the shore.

'This is your heart's home? Dr. Freud asked.

Bruce took in a deep breath and let it out slowly.

'Yes.' I took a picture of Bruce with his painting. 'I'll come back again someday,' he said. 'Spend more time with it. But you were going to show us your painting, Doc. Lead the way.'

Dr. Freud turned to me.

'What about you, Grant?' she said. 'Don't you have a favorite?'

'I haven't seen mine yet.'

She glanced at her watch. 'They'll be up here any minute, to clear us out.'

'Let's go see yours. We've got time. Maybe I'll see mine on the way out.'

She nodded and we followed her, walking briskly. Frankly, the suspense was killing me. What painting was Dr. Freud's favorite? *Whistler's Mother? Nude Descending a Staircase?* What might her favorite painting show us about *her*?

She turned a corner, then walked right up to it. It was stunning. I'd never seen it before. Dr. Freud clasped her hands in front of her, eased her shoulders and smiled.

I went over to the description and noticed that the artist, Marie-Guillemine Benoist, was a woman. A female painter. In 1800. This surprised me. Here was a portrait of a black woman, dressed in a white toga, a turban on her head, with black silk fabric on the chair behind her, looking elegant, staring right back at the viewer. Incredibly life-like. Every detail full of truth. Painted by a French female artist.

'I'm sure you can guess why this painting speaks to me.'

'She kind of looks like you. Her eyes have the same stare. Like she isn't going to take any nonsense from anybody,' Bear said.

Dr. Freud smiled.

'I like it because she is one of the very few faces in this museum that looks anything like me. But I like that it was done by a woman, showing a black woman who appears both powerful and vulnerable at the same time.'

It had finally happened. Dr. Freud was breaking character. She was speaking as Donna now. Not as Freud. That much was clear.

'Yes, she does look powerful,' Joan said, with approval.

'The gaze of the male provokes two emotions in this woman. A protectiveness, a withdrawing from that gaze for self-protection, and a *defiance* of that gaze.'

'Yes,' Bruce said, nodding. 'It's full of rebellion. Like you.'

This comment by Bruce clearly surprised her, as it did me. Our eyes met. Then she went on.

'In 1800, Marie-Guillemine Benoist made the people in power really see this woman, face to face. She presents her in the same pose, same clothes, same attitude as those white

153

women who posed for classical paintings in that day. She was partially unclothed, ... uh... the word...' made into an object?'

'Objectified?' I offered.

'Yes ... objectified for the pleasure of men. But it was a very bold subject matter for that time. Slavery was still legal in the United States and in Britain. She's been here, in Louvre, for over two hundred years, reminding us that these problems still existed.'

I think it was the most words I had heard Dr. Freud say. And it left me speechless. Her English was quite good.

'May I?' I stepped up to the painting and she posed next to it for me, her head held high.

Joan spoke up.

'Liberté, Equality...'

'Humanity,' Madonna said, finishing the phrase.

'Yes,' I said. 'That's better.'

We were interrupted by an announcement over the loudspeakers.

'Please exit the building. It is closing time.' It was repeated in French, German, Italian and English. There was an annoying gong too. A low-key fire alarm.

This had the urgency of a fire drill. People were moving quickly to the stairwells. Uniformed guards appeared in the doorways with arms outstretched, as if they were herding cattle to the exits.

We moved obediently towards the door. And then I saw it.

'Wait! There's mine!' I said. 'Just there.' I moved to another painting by Delacroix. This one was of shoes. Four gorgeous pointy tipped slippers. _Étude de Babouches._

Dr. Freud was giggling.

'What?' I said. 'I like shoes. They're beautiful.'

'Yes. Do you get the pun? You're attracted to beautiful souls.'

'Monsieur! Madame! Merci!' The guards were getting aggressive now. Closing in on us. It seemed we were the last ones in this room. Their white gloved hands outstretched, a whistle on a chain around their necks. These guys were serious. It was time to go.

I turned to see that Madonna and Bruce were there with us, but not Joan or Bear. Seeing my look of distress, Bruce explained.

'They ran downstairs to have one last look at _Liberté_ and the tiger. We can pick them up on the way out. We mustn't forget Statue, either.'

'Right. Let's go.'

We scooted just ahead of our escorts down the stairs. The people in the stairwell sounded like excited birds. All a flutter. For a moment I worried we might lose each other in the crowd going down, but when we peeled away from the river of tourists, I heard shouting coming from the 700 gallery. It was Joan. We ran toward her voice.

When we entered the gallery, she was standing on a bench in the center of the room yelling at the security guards who approached her. They had batons which were raised. Her eyes wild, her body possessed, she had become the leader of armies, filled with the spirit of God. It was Joan of Arc! Bear was waving his burly arms at us, in a panic.

'Liberté, égalité, humanité!' she cried, emphatically. One guard tried to pull at her elbows yelling for her to come down off the bench. But she knocked him sideways, a dynamo of strength. Two more guards were blowing whistles and the room began to fill with them, poised for violence. Bear was being subdued in moments, three men on top of him, but he was fighting back and roaring at them.

Three more guards had managed to pull at Joan's hands and pin them behind her as they dragged her off the bench.

'Get off her!' yelled Bear, breaking free and ploughing into them. A dozen more security guards came after him.

It was a brawl now. In the Louvre. With security.

Bruce instantly became Bruce Lee; his hands and feet were flying in all directions. They tried to grab him, but he was moving too fast.

Dr. Freud was clapping her hands like a school marm, calling for everyone to stop it immediately! Needless to say, no one heard her, and she was grabbed too, pushed against the wall.

Madonna jumped on the back of one of the officers who had Bear pinned down to the ground and was bashing him on the head with her handbag. She screamed at me, 'Take pictures! Take pictures or no one will believe this!'

I saw she was right. Documentation was needed and I pulled my camera up and fired off a dozen shots before I felt a yank at my neck and turned to see a guard trying to take my camera away.

'DON'T! TOUCH! MY! CAMERA!' I screamed and pulled it back towards me. Six more were coming at me, but I saw Marcel waving frantically at me. He was by the door and free of guards. He held out his hands and motioned for me to *throw* him my camera! In an instant, I could see the logic. He could make a dash for the exit with my camera safe in his arms. I took the strap from my neck and hurled it at him. Bless him! He caught it and ran out the door.

Then I was clobbered in the face. The shock of it hit me harder. How could this have gotten so out of hand!

We heard the droning of the police sirens, which made us all pause and look up.

'Run!' yelled Bruce, leaping over two downed guards and out the door. We all pulled ourselves together and ran after him.

We ran like the wind!

Sailing down the stairs, now empty of tourists, we were hotly pursued by the security guards. I didn't look back to see how many, but it sounded like a lot. They came thundering down after us.

When we came to the courtyard where we'd left Statue, we ran by him.

'Come on!' yelled Bear. 'Run!'

I turned to see Statue stick out his foot, causing the guards to trip and fall all over themselves. This bought us valuable time. He caught up with us as we approached the exit. But here is where we met our fate. A row of guards blocked our way with combat gear. The security chief was standing there with him.

'You are all under arrest!' he barked.

'On what charge!' cried Dr. Freud, hands on hips, like a trial lawyer, all of a sudden, in a court case.

'Disturbing the public peace in the Louvre!'

'Those idiots attacked her!' Bear growled as he pointed to the guards, who all started talking at once to the director. But he shushed them with one finger in the air.

'My guards know better than to lay a hand on you.'

'Well, I got it on film!' I cried, feeling victorious. 'Those guards were using force! They may have injured my friend here.'

Then the director stepped forward, his eyes glued on the camera that Marcel held.

'Give it here.' He held his hands out.

Marcel put it behind his back like a recalcitrant child and shook his head.

'That's my property!' I yelled. 'I'm an American citizen.'

This gave him pause.

'And he has a plane to catch!' cried Madonna. Though I'm not sure that did us any favors.

The man was smiling.

'I'll tell you what I'll do then. I'm going to confiscate that camera, as is my right, because you were using a flash when taking pictures. It says clearly on our website, that you are not allowed to take flash pictures. You all saw flash, did you not?' he cried to his thugs.

'Yes, Sir!' They snapped to attention.

'That's a lie!' I yelled.

'Give me the camera, and I'll let you all go. If not, I will have you all arrested and you will spend the night in jail.'

We all gasped. Even Statue.

'I can't give up my camera,' I yelled. I was really losing it. Sweat dripping from my forehead. I had kept all the pictures on the camera card. No backups. I didn't have a computer with me. 'This camera is digital. It has all my photographs on it. A month's worth of work! I was here in Paris on assignment—'

'You should have thought of that when making trouble at the Louvre.'

All eyes were on me. I couldn't let this happen. Not to me. Not to my friends. Not to my work. The best work of my life!

Then Marcel walked slowly toward the director, with his arms extended, holding the camera before him like a dead animal.

'No! Don't do it, Marcel!' cried Madonna.

The rest of them moaned and tried to reach for it, but I could see it was the only answer. Marcel was right. I knew this director would destroy the images on my camera to save his own skin. There'd be nothing left. All that hard work. Gone. But I didn't relish spending a night in a French prison and I worried what they might do to Joan. They might take her somewhere else.

'Do it, Marcel. Give it to him.'

Marcel hung his head and held it out with both hands. Two officers came and took my Nikon D7 away. My talisman. My magic. I was feeling faint. Like I might just pass out.

The security guards herded us through an open the door and we were told quite plainly to scram and never come back. In intense, colorful French.

As we filed out the door, I could hear Joan weeping.

When we were all safely outside, she hung on my neck.

'I'm so sorry, Grant! This is all my fault! Your lovely pictures!'

'Not your fault,' I said, wiping my eyes. 'They were out of line. They wanted the evidence against their behavior. It was just bad luck. I can get a new camera.'

'Grant has to catch his plane,' Bruce said. He turned and made a few parting obscene gestures at the guards who were still staring us down from the glass door. This, of course, put them in a frothing fit.

We all turned and walked away fast toward to the big plaza. No one said a word. The shock of it all was still fresh, until Madonna cried out, 'Well look who it is!' and pointed toward the boulevard.

A figure came hurdling toward us on a bicycle, peddling fast.

I laughed despite my heartache. 'Christ on a bike!'

It was JC. She came skidding to a stop and hopped off.

'What are you doing here?' I asked.

'I just got a feeling you might need a little help.'

'You were right!'

'I work in mysterious ways. Now hurry up or you'll miss your plane! Take this bike. Now go! You can call a taxi to pick you up at your flat.'

I drew her to me in a big American hug.

'We got in a big fight with the guards at the Louvre and ... and they took Grant's camera!' wailed Joan, still indignant.

JC's eyes locked with mine in concern.

'Oh, Grant! Your pictures!'

'They would have arrested us if I didn't let them take it.'

'Oh, darling! You made a sacrifice!'

Then Marcel sauntered up to me and tapped me on the shoulder. He dug in his pocket for something and pulled it out. In the palm of his hand was the memory card from my Nikon D 70. The genius!

'When did you get this?' I asked, baffled.

He mimed running ahead of me, stopping, and taking it out.

'Clever man! Marcel! Thank you! I still have the pictures then!'

Everyone cheered. The relief was enormous. All was not lost. Dr Freud now raised her hand and we quieted.

'I will return tomorrow and demand the camera back. If they don't give it to me, I'll threaten to publish the pictures online. They'll have to give it back. It's no good to them without the pictures,' she said.

'We can send it on to you. You gave us your address,' Madonna said, a big smile on her face. She took my hand and squeezed it.

'So, I did. That would be wonderful. Thank you.'

We formed a circle and put our arms around each other.

'Merci,' I said. But there was so much more I couldn't find the words for. The pictures would have to do.

Chapter Thirteen

I wasn't in the air fifteen minutes before I was missing my friends – and French croissants. It's not easy to get good croissants in Cornwall, or any place else in England, for that matter. And crêpes? Marie's crêpes? Forget about it. Thus, it was with pangs of regret that I gripped my armrests, then tried to shift my attention from feelings of loss to gratitude. I picked up the book by Thich Naht Hahn, the one Katie had given me, on meditation. I was thinking I should give it a try when I got back.

They were closing the gate when I rushed up, out of breath, waving my boarding pass. It was closer than I would have liked it to be, but traffic in Paris is terrible! Even on a bike. I would never have made it if it hadn't been for JC and her inspired bike. I wondered where she'd got it. She said she'd pick it up at my flat later. I said Madame Garnier would have it for her. It wasn't as hip a bike as Indigo's, but it got me to my place where I could call the taxi and throw my stuff in my bag. It was an expensive ride but saved me the trauma of another train ride and revisiting my original experience of the train stations and the pickpockets. I almost wished I'd had the time to go back that way, to show myself that I'd conquered that fear. Yeah, Paris was a big city. I'd learned things from it.

I'd seen the glamor, the lights, the landmarks, the attraction of the best of everything. I'd seen the glamorous people too. And where the rich and famous hang out. Madonna had pointed out a restaurant on the top of one old building where people flew in from Dallas, Texas to have dinner there for 2000 euros. Just one meal! But that sort of stuff didn't interest me all that much. What drew me were the vagabonds, the crêpe makers, the performers. Madonna, Bruce, Statue, Marcel, Bear, Joan, Dr. Freud, and JC. Just people, struggling to have a life in Paris. People with talents and troubles. Who were one thing on the outside and another on the inside. Like the rest of us.

I came to Paris as a stranger. Hopeful, in my ignorance, but then fearful because of my experience. Everything I thought I understood about to navigate in the world was turned on its head. Without language, I wasn't sure of anything. I was lucky I had a lifeboat. A back up. A credit line. Ron. I was lucky to have a friend like Leslie who gave me her flat to live in for a month and was lucky my new friends spoke English.

When I finally got on UK ground again, I took a night's sleep in an airport hotel. Then I made the seven-hour journey back to my little house by the sea and my waiting family, I kissed my wife and my daughter and even grabbed Cassandra and kissed her too. She took a swipe at me that caused general hilarity and I thanked my lucky stars for the sound of that laughter. I saw both my wife and daughter with new eyes and could have sworn Ariel had grown while I was gone.

'I'm so glad you're home, Daddy,' she said. 'You were gone so long!'

'Did it seem like years?'

'A THOUSAND years!'

I tickled her.

'I have something to ask you,' I said.

'Go on.'

She sat on the floor of her bedroom, legs folded at what seemed to me impossible angles.

'I hear they've been teaching you how to meditate at school. Can you teach me?'

Ariel narrowed her eyes, studying me and my potential as a devotee of meditation.

'I don't know everything about it,' she said, judiciously. 'But I can show you some things.'

'Great.'

I sat down next to her.

She made me put my hands on the floor next to her, raise my butt in the air and rise on my toes.

'Stretches. To start.'

'uhhhhhuh...' I was holding my breath in concentration.

'Let the breath out, Daddy. Just stretch.'

'Right!'

I collapsed. As a six-foot Daddy is wont to do.

'Now sit like this.'

She demonstrated a beautiful cross-legged position with her hands on her knees, index fingers touching thumbs. Her eyes were closed, but I watched her carefully and made an effort. She peeked and smiled.

'Good!'

'Really?'

'You'll get better. With practice.'

Chapter Fourteen

The fact that my favorite pub in St. Ives was called the Golden Lion, now had a new significance. Seeing my buddies again there was a sweet reunion. Besides hanging out there together, we also played in a band. I played the spoons. Ed and Todd were on fiddle, Jonesy the pipes. We performed once a month at the pub and had a great time doing it. I had to miss our monthly performance, but they reluctantly forgave me, complaining that the summer months were when they got the most tips.

When I finally brought in some of my best pictures to show them—glossy, eight by ten, black and white prints, they poured over them and I suffered the full range of their sneers and laughter until I held my hands up.

'Hold on, now. There are stories that go with these.'

'I should hope so,' Pete said. 'These look like strange people, mate.'

It had taken eight years for Pete to call me mate. For most of that time, I was 'the American.' It took a long time for these guys in St. Ives, mostly fishermen, to trust what was not familiar. The people in these pictures were foreigners to them. And this lot were not used to looking at photography as 'art.'

'My assignment was to explore what interested me,' I tried to explain.

'What? Men dressed as Madonna?'

I bit my lips.

'That's my friend, you're talking about, Pete. Have some respect. He looked out for me in a strange place. Protected me. I owe him a lot.'

Pete frowned but nodded. He understood loyalty.

'Who's this guy?' Jim asked.

'That's Bear.'

'Looks like a bear, doesn't he?'

They all made noises of agreement.

'He's the one who showed me the lion in the cage.'

'Poor thing. That isn't right. It's a shame,' Tim said. 'A creature like that.'

'Hey, I have an idea, Grant,' Pete said. 'You know how we had a show here with your pictures from China? Let's do another one of your photographs from Paris and let's try to raise some money for that lion to find a new home.'

A cheer came from everyone in the pub.

'Free the Golden Lion!'

Once the noise died down, we got to particulars. A date was arranged with the owner, Ted.

'Can we actually do something about that lion in Paris?' John asked. His hard black eyes focused on me.

'As a matter of fact, I've been doing some hunting around about that. And there is a charity in France, working on relocating the lion to a modern zoo, one with no cages. I don't see why we couldn't contribute to it.'

I pulled it up on my phone, the particular charity, and showed them. Nods all around as I copied the email address.

Just to be sure, I asked Katie, that night, my lawyer wife.

'Doesn't hurt to email and ask,' she said. 'I bet Leslie will love the idea.'

~

Leslie did. She made good on her word to do an article about my trip in *Cornwall Now* and it included the promotion of my show of photographs at *The Golden Lion* in St. Ives. We charged at the door for the photography show and several people bought prints. We raised £400 and sent it off to the charity.

My camera came back to me by post along with eight self-portraits done in crayon by my friends from the Pompidou, which were included in the show. I sent them each a magazine and a report on what we raised for the liberation of the lion. I could imagine Joan being particularly proud. I also imagined them laughing together over a pizza lunch on the piazza. I was glad to have my pictures of them to remind me of the way I was changed by Paris.

Acknowledgements:

My thanks go to Stephen van Dulken, my husband – for his faith, love, support, and proofreading. Thanks to family and dear friends for their encouragement, to alpha readers Kathie Nielsen, Deirdre Gainor, and Raphaël Neal. Thank you, Tanja Slijepčević, for your patient assistance and for the great work done by the whole team at Books Go Social. I appreciated the editing help of Jacqui Lofthouse. Thank you to my grandson, Indigo Jack Erikson Foley for his inspiration and meditation lessons.

Thanks to readers everywhere, to supporters of my books and all books, to independent bookstores and to the creative community in Hastings and St Leonards for the continuous flow of inspiration and connection.

A Paris Odyssey by Axel Forrester is a work of fiction, autobiography, and dream. Much of what is presented are memories of my trip to Paris in 2001. I got a grant to explore Paris with my cameras and some of that work became the art installation 'Passages' and appeared in another installation called 'Traumbagger' with Lise Patt.

Book cover design by Axel Forrester
To see photography from my Paris trip in 2001, visit my Instagram account for the Odyssey series.
@acornishodyssey

www.axelforrester.com

A Cornish Odyssey by Axel Forrester is the first in the Odyssey series.

"Funny, poignant, each chapter a surprise, as this young man not only discovers the magic of Cornwall, but the magic inherently in him." - Deidre Gainor

A humorous, fish out of water story, this page-turner is a delight, a romp through Cornwall that will make you laugh out loud and leave you wanting more. If you like Bill Bryson you'll enjoy this writing. It entertains while taking you on a journey. This novella is a love letter to Cornwall and its quirky characters.

Grant Decker is a disgruntled California art teacher turned 40, who has lost his way in life. A random stab on the map means he's going to Penzance to spend his school holiday, hiking around the coast of Cornwall. Everything about Cornwall is strange to this American—the accents, the food, the changing weather. Determined to show Graeme, his trip planner, he's not a lazy American, he avoids the bus and crashes through the scenery with comic effect. Walking on the coastal path he has visions of pirates, saints, mermaids, and chocolate cake, but it's through his encounters with the people of Cornwall that he learns how to be his authentic self.

You can find **A Cornish Odyssey** at The Hastings Bookshop in Hastings, UK, Hare and Hawthorn Bookshop in Hastings, Eastgate Bookshop in Devon, Mr B's Emporium of Reading Delights in Bath, or you can order it at just about any bookshop or find it on Amazon. The audiobook, narrated by Danny Horn, is available where audiobooks are sold online.

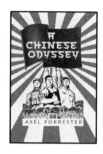

A Chinese Odyssey by Axel Forrester is the second book in the series.

'...filled with a plethora of interesting characters,' **International Review of Books**

'Well written with details of the trials and tribulations of the protagonist, Grant Decker. I was riveted. A totally fun and enjoyable read.' **Elaine Appel**

It is 2010 and American Grant Decker is living his dream of being a photographer in Cornwall. He's got a chance to go to China, courtesy of Charon, his ex-girlfriend. What she hasn't told him is that the trip, with a group of American teachers, includes a risky plan that could bring the wrath of the Chinese government upon him. He slips and slides through a packed itinerary encountering places and people that surprise him – people like Guy Anderson, Dr Sòng, the Mosuo people and the Chinese barber/musicians in Dali who will remain in his memory forever. Despite restrictions, he manages to take some of the best pictures of his life and make his escape with a bit of help from a witchy connection in St Ives. With the same highly readable prose as the first book, **A Cornish Odyssey**, join Grant in a new round of engaging and funny adventures.

Reviewed in the United Kingdom on 12 November 2022

'This was a brilliant read. I really couldn't put this short novel down and had to read it all in one sitting. It was a fantastic story line that was both interesting and exciting. The characters were great and realistic. I love the way this book is half fiction and part autobiographical. It really made it feel like a very real story. I was certainly engrossed in reading it as it was so well written. This book was certainly close to getting that 5th star. I would have loved for this book to be much longer as I was gutted when it ended. China is certainly a very complex and fascinating country. I felt like I had learnt so much from reading this book. I certainly recommend reading this book if you love travelling the world through fictional books. It contains some wonderful culture. I am interested in reading more books by this great author. So much praise goes out to the author and publishing team for creating this interesting and believable story.'

A Chinese Odyssey can also be found and ordered through independent and traditional bookstores and Amazon.